D1109957

14 STORIES

STEPHEN DIXON

14
STORIES

THE JOHNS HOPKINS UNIVERSITY PRESS
BALTIMORE AND LONDON

This book has been brought to publication with the generous assistance of the G. Harry Pouder Fund.

Originally published, 1980
Second printing, 1989

Grateful acknowledgment is made to the following publications for permission to reprint the following stories, all of which appear in somewhat different form:
"14 Stories" originally appeared in *Pequod.* "Signatures" appeared in different versions in *Gallimaufry* and the *Ohio Journal* (Autumn 1977). "Milk Is Very Good for You" appeared in *Quarry West* and *Pushcart Prize II.* "The Sub" originally appeared in the *Remington Review.* "The Signing" originally appeared in *North American Review.* "Love Has Its Own Action" originally appeared in *Transatlantic Review.* "Cut" originally appeared in *Quarry West.* "Out of Work" originally appeared in the *Antioch Review.* "The Intruder" originally appeared in *Fiction.* "Ann from the Street" originally appeared in *Confrontation.* "Names" originally appeared in the *Georgia Review.* "Streets" originally appeared in *Harper's Magazine.*

The Johns Hopkins University Press
701 West 40th Street
Baltimore, Maryland 21211
The Johns Hopkins Press Ltd., London

Library of Congress Cataloging in Publication Data
Dixon, Stephen, 1936–
   14 stories.

   (Johns Hopkins, poetry and fiction)
   I. Title. II. Series.
PZ4.D6217Fo [PS3554.I92] 813'.54 80–14911
ISBN 0–8018–2445–1

To my brother Don

ACADEMIC

CONTENTS

14 STORIES   1

SIGNATURES   17

MILK IS VERY GOOD FOR YOU   23

THE SUB   36

THE SIGNING   54

THE SECURITY GUARD   59

LOVE HAS ITS OWN ACTION   74

CUT   87

OUT OF WORK   103

THE INTRUDER   112

ANN FROM THE STREET   121

NAMES   126

STREETS   134

14 STORIES

14 STORIES

Eugene Randall held the gun in front of his mouth and fired. The bullet smashed his upper front teeth, left his head through the back of his jaw, pierced an ear lobe and broke a window that overlooked much of the midtown area. A chambermaid on the floor said to herself "What kind of noise is that— that sounds like a bullet. And a window being broke. But maybe it wasn't either." The bullet landed a block away on a brownstone roof, where a boy was watching mama-and-papa pigeons sitting in the sun. Mr. Randall fell over the end table, sending to the floor a lamp, pack of cigarillos and an ashtray that had been resting on the three notes he'd written regarding his suicide. The wind came in through the broken window, picked the letters off the floor and distributed them around the room. The chambermaid leaned on her cleaning cart and said "Yes sir, that was a shot all right. Someone's practicing on the windows or furniture or maybe gone and killed himself or someone he didn't like. It happened last month on the twenty-first. And a year before that on the eighth. All kinds of suicides and nuts end up in this hotel, and these drunken conventioneers and lonely Japanese businessmen the worst." She lifted a phone receiver. One letter landed on the couch. Another under the coffee table. The

1

third floated out the window and higher than Mr. Randall's room on the fourteenth floor. The boy looked at the bullet that had rolled to within a foot of him. He thought it was a stone, picked it up, dropped it because it felt so rough, almost prickly, stared at it and said "Holy G, that's a bullet. Someone tried to shoot me with a bullet," and opened the roof door and ran downstairs. The pigeons flapped when the door slammed behind the boy, settled in the same positions they were in before. "This is Anna," the chambermaid said on the phone, "Anna from the fourteenth, and I think there's been a shooting on my floor." The hotel detective said maybe it was a loud car backfire she'd heard and Anna said "No sir, no backfire. I heard it while in the hallway, so you could be right if you said it came from a guest's television screen." He told her to wait for him by the center elevators and she said "Make it snappy, sir, as who's to say there isn't a lunatic loose."

Mr. Randall lay groaning on the floor. Bad shot, bad shot, he thought, he tried to say. That note out the window—which one?— he hoped not to his ex-wife or mother.

"Where's the fire?" a neighbor said, grabbing the boy's arm as he raced around the second-story landing.

"Someone tried to kill me up there—with a bullet. I was sitting watching the pigeons, minding my business, when wham, it's shot, a bullet, not an inch from my eye. If I'd been sitting where I always sit, I'd be dead, I swear."

"Now what kind of story is that?" the neighbor said, and the boy said "You want to come and see?" and they went up to the roof. The neighbor pushed open the door slowly, said it was safe, no sharpshooting assassins from what he could see, "that is, if you're telling the truth," and stepped onto the roof.

"There it is," the boy said, pointing to the bullet between their feet. "Don't touch it. The police will want it for evidence." The man picked up the bullet. "I said not to touch it. You're going to get in trouble. The police don't like people fooling with their evidence."

"Don't worry." The neighbor inspected the bullet. "This is a bullet all right. No little air pellet either. It's a real bullet, real meaning from a real pistol or rifle, probably a .22. You're lucky you're alive." They went downstairs to phone the police.

"Right this way, sir," Anna said to the hotel detective who came out of the elevator. "Right down here somewhere down this hall's where I heard the bullet sound." The detective said he would check out her story with some guests on the floor and knocked on the first of the twenty rooms in this wing of the hotel.

"Yes?" a male guest said through the peephole, and the detective identified himself, said don't be alarmed but wondered if the guest had heard anything around here in the last fifteen minutes that sounded like a gun being fired.

"A gun? No, not since breakfast. No, let me correct that—not since a few seconds after the boy wheeled in my breakfast. I shot him for bringing me three two-minute eggs when I had explicitly called down for two three's."

"Thank you very much," the detective said and Anna and he went to the next door. Nobody answered. He let himself in with a passkey. No smell, no bullet, no disturbance here, he thought. And nice neat person who's renting the place also—pants hung so evenly over the back of the chair, the orderly way he put his toilet and personal articles on the dresser, all lined up like a column of soldiers. "Let's try the next one," he said.

Head, pain, help, quick, Mr. Randall thought. He tried to scream. He tried to crawl. He tried to reach for a part of the broken lamp to throw and smash so someone would hear the noise and come. But his arms and fingers wouldn't move. His lips did, but nothing came out but more blood and pain. Better in a hospital. Better under sedation. Anything better than this, this pain, this killing pain.

"Maybe I ought to tell my mom first," the boy said, stopping on the fourth floor. He didn't know whether to ring the bell so his mother could have time to fix herself or open the door with his key and maybe surprise her nude or in panties, which she didn't mind when they were alone, but with this man with him and all. . . . "Maybe I better ring," the boy said.

3

"Don't you have a key to your own place? You seem old enough."

"Who said I didn't?" He unlocked the door, parted it an inch, yelled "Hey mom—you home?" though he knew she was, reading or asleep. She only went out on Fridays, to shop.

The wind died and the note drifted for a while over a busy street before it landed on the hood of a parked car. A young woman walking arm in arm with a man said "Look, Ron, a message from heaven just came." She started for the car but the man, keeping their arms locked at the elbows and spreading his feet to anchor his weight, jerked her back to his side. "Let me get it," she said. "Maybe it'll tell us where a secret city fortune is."

"Uh-uh," Ron said. "We're chained like this for life."

"For life—that's nice." She kissed his lips. "Though it also sounds horrid, like a prison term. But please let me see what it says."

"Well. . . why don't we kind of slide over there together." They moved sideways, arms still locked, the woman leading, till she got close enough to stretch for the note with her free hand, but it was blown over the car hood. "This is getting exciting," she said, and they waited for the traffic to pass so they could follow the note across the street.

Mr. Randall couldn't move his body from the waist up. He was able to dig his knees into the carpet and push himself a few inches a minute that way, but even if he reached the door he wouldn't be able to unfasten the latch or turn the knob. He would be able to draw attention by banging the door with his feet, but it might take him an hour to get there. He didn't want to suddenly get stiff in his haul across the room and then suffer this pain for hours till he died. Better the telephone on the end table at the other side of the couch. He could knee himself there, knock the table over with his feet. The operator would know something was wrong when no one answered. And if he got his mouth right on the receiver she would hear him breathing.

"What is it, love?" the boy's mother said, coming out of the bedroom. "Oh, excuse me," and she turned and quickly buttoned up her bathrobe. "You should've told me you were with someone, Warren."

"It was sort of emergency—that's why I forgot."

The man was thinking And I always thought she was so flat and skinny, I don't know why. Seen her on the stairs maybe three four times in a year and always thought she had a body like a boy and even looked like one with her short hair and always sneakers and slacks. But good Christ what a figure.

"I was up on the roof watching the pigeons when someone tried to shoot me, ma."

"Something like that, Mrs. Lang. I was climbing the steps when Warren was running down, and I asked what was wrong and he said the same thing he told you. Here it is," and he opened his fist and showed her the bullet.

"You sure he didn't just plant that thing up there? You didn't, did you, Warren?"

"Well because of his frightened look when he was running down, I tended to believe him. Nobody could impersonate such a scare—not even an actor. You think you should call the police?"

"My God, what a neighborhood. Boys being shot at on roofs. Shopkeepers hiring police dogs. Addicts, these filthy addicts making us all fearful to walk into our own homes. Are you sure that's a bullet—what's your name, please?"

"William Singerton. I'm a neighbor, one floor right below you. In fact, we have the exact same apartment layout I see, though your stove and refrigerator are bigger."

"If you think his story's authentic, Mr. Singerton. I mean, even if someone was only shooting the pigeons, I suppose you should still call the police." Mr. Singerton dialed Operator.

"Hear that?" the hotel detective said.

"Hear what?" Anna said.

"Phone falling. I heard the short tingling like from the bell inside a phone when it falls. Came from one of the rooms down there," and they walked to the three doors at the end of the corridor.

"'Dear Mom,' the letter starts off with," the young woman said. "It's to this Gene fellow's mother, and the writing seems very legible and intelligent."

"Let me see," Ron said.

"First you got to let go of my arm."

"I told you, Loey: we're locked like this forever and ever no matter what adversities we face. Now let me see the letter."

"Not till you release me."

"I'll release you if you kiss me once on the cheek, once where my eyebrows meet, and once right here, smack dab on it," and he touched his lips.

She kissed him on all three spots. "Now release me."

"Not until you hand me the letter. Because what I failed to mention about me is also your main disadvantage: you're linked for life to a liar."

"Then neither of us is going to read it," and she stuck the letter into her coat pocket.

"Hello? I said, hello? I said, this is Mrs. Vega, your hotel operator, may I help you?" She signaled the operator seated beside her to remove her earphones. "What should I do? 1403's breathing pretty heavy into the receiver but not answering me."

"Maybe they accidentally knocked over the phone while they were making love. That happens. Check with Desk if it's a couple staying there, or someone with a small child."

"What should I tell the breather?"

"Say 'Hold on,' that's all. 'Hold on' and then call down and ask who's in 1403. Also ask if the guest's got a dog or cat, which could also be the problem."

"Thanks, Andrea. I only hope I can be as much help to the girl who takes over from me when I go."

"The girl who takes over from you is going to be a machine, dearie—a computer with a recorded sweet voice and perfect brain. Why do you think I'm leaving the profession after so long? Not only because you never meet anyone but the janitor, cooped up in this cell, but for another reason that the job's getting extinct. For you it's fine because you need a couple years' wages till your husband says 'Let's have a baby.' But for me, a lifetime worker—I know that, there's no family or man in my future—this profession's dying out quickly. Like the ink pen. Like the elevator operator."

"Like the elevator operator. That's true. They haven't any in this hotel, do they?" and she rang the desk clerk.

"A phone drop?" the woman guest in 1402 said. "Since when does management have to send up a detective to see about a phone being dropped?"

"It's related to something else—a possible accident on the floor."

She called out "Leonard? Did you recently drop a telephone on the floor?" and a man yelled back through the closed bathroom door "Not unless I did and didn't know about it."

"What's the trouble if I may ask?" the woman said. "I'm worried now."

"Don't be. It's only that Anna here—"

"How do you do, ma'am," Anna said.

"Anna thought she heard a noise like a gunshot go off before, though it could have been a car backfire or sound effects from a TV show."

"Leonard," she yelled, "did you hear anything like a gunshot before? Something that wasn't a car backfiring or from a television show?"

"I did," Leonard said through the door. "From right where I'm sitting. But I didn't know what to figure with this town, so I forgot about it. Why, is someone hurt?"

Over the phone the desk sergeant took down the name, address, apartment and telephone number of Mrs. Lang. "You sure some-one will be home when we get there?" he said.

"We'll stay here till the police come," Mr. Singerton said.

"What's your connection with the mother and the boy?"

"A neighbor."

"A neighbor around the neighborhood, in the building or a roomer in Mrs. Lang's apartment?"

"In the building, though I don't see what bearing that has on the matter. When the questions get that personal I sort of feel I shouldn't have gotten involved."

"All right," the sergeant said. "Just stay where you are and a man will be right over. And don't touch the bullet. Leave everything in its place."

"He said not to touch the bullet," Mr. Singerton said to Mrs. Lang, opening his fist and showing her the bullet. "What do you think they'll do when they find out I did?"

"Why don't you put it back where you found it?" Warren said.

"With my prints all over it? Besides, if they find out, I'll get in more trouble that way."

"Wipe them off why don't you, but I told you not to touch it."

"Thank you. *He told me.* If I'd been smart I should have let him pass when he came flying downstairs. I never should have left my flat for cigarettes—never should have been smoking, in fact. Cancer I'll get, and also a jail sentence. In fact, I never should have taken my first puff when I was young and everyone said don't take your first puff, Willy, because it will lead to bad things. Little did they know. Do you smoke, Warren?"

"Me? I'm only ten."

"Well don't, you hear? Don't even experiment. Take my troubles with the police now as an example why not to."

"'Dear Mom,'" Loey read. "'I'm sorry for what sadness to you and disrespect for the family my death this way will cause you, but all I ask is that you try not to be too sad and try to understand me. I've thought about killing myself for more than a year now. I tried to work things out for myself many other ways, but everything I did always made things even worse, which you know for me is really not too hard to believe. After the business went, Sarah and the kids went soon after that and it was just too much for me. And then all my so-called friends went. I suppose they thought I'd sponge on them or else be too maudlin a person to be with, now that my business and wife and—' I can't go on," Loey said. She gave the note to Ron, began crying. He unhooked his arm from hers and said "Maybe this letter isn't a joke at all."

"You mean you still think someone could think up a joke like that?"

"Yes."

"But the letter writer even put his mother's name, address, city, state and phone number on top of the page. Now why would a joker go to that far extent in making a joke?"

"To make the joke seem more real?"

"He'd write a long letter like this and put all that information about a woman on top of the page and then sail it out the window hoping that someone he had never seen before and would never see unless he's now looking at us from one of those windows, would find the note and think the suicide story is real?"

"I didn't say I was positive it was a joke. I only said I maybe still think it is." He read the note: "' . . . too maudlin a person' etcetera, 'children were gone,' period. 'I don't know. I can't explain anything anymore. I'm sick. Blame the whole affair on my emotional sickness. I'm sorry, mom. I love you. I hate for the pain I know I'm going to inflict on you. You've been the dearest person in my life. Of course Greta and Zane are dear, but they're across the country and too young to help. This note's too long. I love you, mom. It's silly, but if I could live it would be most to spare you the pain of my death. I was almost going to say "To help you live through the pain of my death," which is why I said before "It's silly." And now I'm getting too silly for a suicide note, besides too long. Always my love. Your devoted son, Gene.'"

"The note's real," Ron said. "I feel awful feeling it wasn't. I think we should call the police about this, as that mother should get her note."

"No she shouldn't," Loey said, and grabbed the note from him and tore it up and threw the pieces in the gutter. She ran across the street and around the corner.

"There's a Mr. Eugene A. Randall in 1403," the desk clerk told the operator on the phone. "It's a double occupancy he's in, and though he's renting it as such, he's a single."

"Well I hate to be a busybody, Mr. Hire. But 1403's been buzzing me for some time now, and when I said 'Hello, may I help you?' all I heard was heavy breathing."

"Is that room still on the line?"

She switched 1403 off Hold, heard the same kind of heavy breathing, said "Hello? Mr. Randall? This is Mrs. Vega again, your hotel operator. Is anything wrong? I said, is anything wrong?" She switched 1403 to Hold and said "Still on it, Mr. Hire, breathing just as regularly. Being new here I don't want to be advising you your business, but I really think something's the matter."

Mr. Hire dialed the hotel detective's extension, but nobody was in. He checked in his book of private listings, called Operator and told her to page Detective Feuer on his pocket pager and have him contact Mr. Hire on extension 78 regarding a possible hotel accident.

"Hello?" Mrs. Vega said in his head, "is anything the matter, 1403? If it is then say so. Say 'Help' if you can't say anything else. Well if this is Mr. Randall and anything is wrong with you, then someone's coming right up, Mr. Randall. I'm sure they'll be right there."

Someone knocked, rang the bell. "Mr. Randall, you in?" a man said. "Better use the passkey," another man said. "What did he look like?" the first man said. "I don't know," a woman said, "I never saw him. When I brought him his towels, he was in the bedroom. When I brought up glasses and ice for whiskey, he was in the bathroom. He left a good tip both times, though. And never any noise from him till now, sir." The door opened. Lots of legs and stockings and shoes. "Oh God," the woman said. "Oh God, oh God," and she ran screaming down the long hall. She knocked over her cleaning cart. Doors in the corridor opened, heads looked out. "What's all the commotion about?" a woman guest said. "What's with this hotel?" a male guest said. "Noisy—the worst," and he slammed his door. "The doctor will be here shortly, Mr. Randall," a man kneeling beside him said. I'm the hotel manager. Try and rest. Don't speak."

"Now you say you picked up this bullet on the roof here?" the policeman said.

"I didn't pick it up," Warren said. "He did," pointing to Mr. Singerton. "I told him not to, but he wouldn't listen."

"You should have known better, Mr. Singerton."

"I probably did, but got overeager. I wanted to see if the boy was telling the truth. If the bullet was warm, recently fired."

"The sun—lots of things could have warmed it. Not hoping there's a next time—please be more careful? For now I'll report it, and if anything comes in about a shooting here around the time Warren mentioned, then your phoning might be some use." He got up. "Thanks for the coffee, Mrs. Lang."

"Not at all. You finished also, Mr. Singerton?"

"Finished." He handed her his mug, gave a dirty look to Warren.

"I'm sorry," Warren said to him. "I forgot."

"Forgot what?" the policeman said.

"Oh, I forgot I wasn't supposed to say anything about how I wasn't supposed to tell him how I told him not to touch the bullet on the roof. That it was evidence."

Ron caught up with Loey in a drugstore. She was sitting at the counter spooning the whipped cream off a hot chocolate into her mouth. He sat beside her, showed a handful of pieces of torn note. "I think I got every one of them. And I still believe his mother should get it."

"Let's forget we ever read it, Ron. Ever found it?"

"How? Just by pushing it out of our heads? And why try and forget something that maybe really is a joke and now an even bigger one on us because we took it so seriously. And then maybe the man who wrote it was telling the truth but hasn't killed himself yet. I just thought of that. Maybe he's right this moment planning to kill himself tonight or tomorrow morning and this note fell out of his pocket and by phoning the police we can still stop him. That is, if it isn't a joke."

"It isn't a joke."

The fountain man said "Did I hear you say something about someone's suicide note?"

"Not mine or hers, or maybe nobody's. We're not sure. You have a phone we can call the police on?"

"Go through the rear door there into the hotel lobby. They got plenty, all supervised. Ours have all been ripped or kicked out."

"A man, you should've seen him," Anna said in the female employees' washroom. "Room an ugly mess, blood all over his face, a black hole in the side of his cheek, half his ear off as all chewed through. I saw it once and ran as I never did. A Mr. Randall."

"Randall?" a typist in Accounting said. "No, I didn't see his bill today. What room number?"

"1403. Such a clean nice man. I never saw him once since his two days here, but he gave me big tips all the times I came in his room. Once for extra towels. He yelled out to me from the bedroom he liked to bathe a lot. And a second for glasses and ice for whiskey.

And one more time just now I remember. What was it again? He called Service to bring up two real down or no-rubber pillows, and he tipped me for that also. Left the money right where the used whiskey glasses were."

"That's something I've always been curious about. Because I can't see how you girls can know for sure what change lying around when you're cleaning up is for a tip and what change was left by mistake."

"We don't. But if you want to make enough living at our job, then you have to think all change lying around except on the bed or dresser, if all his other pocket things are there also, is yours. That is, if there's only one pile of change and it doesn't come up to a lot more than a dollar for one day let's say, but just to around fifty to a dollar in cents. But if it has odd pennies in the change, meaning one to four but not five or ten exact, then we also don't take. Then we think the change was left by accident, because no tipper leaves odd pennies."

Easy, *easy*, EASY, Mr. Randall thought as he was being lifted onto the stretcher. He wanted to say they were handling his head much too roughly, wheeling the stretcher much too hard. "Easy," he finally said, "or I die."

"Were you planning anything for dinner tonight?" Mr. Singerton said.

"Same as always: something nothing for Warren and me."

"Like to eat out then? This might seem strange—how it started off I mean—though I have seen you on the stairway."

"Seen you also. You must work nights, because the only times I've seen you is during the day."

"I write technical brochures, so I can work home as long as I hand in my copy at the specified time."

"To work in your apartment and get well paid for it would be the best kind of work I'd like to do. But I don't know anything about writing except for letters. Plus a journal I've been keeping on and off since Warren was born."

"To me the worst thing about other people's journals is that I can't read them. I'm a born snoop."

"That's probably why you picked up the bullet when Warren told you not to."

"I knew it had to be something," Warren said.

"You still want to go out?" Mr. Singerton said. "I can pick you up at six."

"That's foolish," she said. "If I lived below you then I could see you coming to my door, but not when I'm one floor above. I'll ring your bell when I'm ready."

"But that wouldn't be proper," he said.

"First saw it on the car hood," Ron said on the phone, "just laying there. It's a bit ripped up now, but I got all the pieces and with Scotch tape I think you could read it. My girlfriend just didn't want to believe the note. Did the guy die?"

"Last we heard, he was living," the detective said. "You stay there and I'll have a man get the note."

"He's still alive," Ron said to Loey. "Shot himself right in the head. I wonder what kind of gun he used."

She grabbed most of the note which Ron had assembled on the counter, and ran out of the drugstore. Ron ran after her, shouted "You crazy? You want us both thrown in jail? The cops have my name. They're coming now to get the note. Bring it back, goddamn you," but she got in a cab and one by one threw the pieces out of the window as the car drove away.

"Goodbye, Mr. Randall," the intern said in the ambulance, and covered Mr. Randall's face with the top of the blanket.

"You were right, Bonnie," Andrea said, removing her earphones. "Desk phoned for me to locate fourteenth-floor service to clean up 1403. That Mr. Randall. A suicide."

Bonnie closed her eyes, was silent, tears came, said "I knew it. That breathing wasn't natural. It didn't sound like sleep or sex or dogs, cats or anything. It truly sounded like someone dying," and she imitated the sounds she heard on the phone. "Like that."

"If you ask me it still sounds like sex," Andrea said. She rang fourteenth-floor service and got Anna on the phone. "Anna, this is Andrea. Mr. Hire wants for you to go to 1403 and clean up the room. I'm sorry, but there's been a suicide there, love." Anna hung up. Andrea called back. "Anna, you feeling sick from what I told you? You see, Mr. Hire wants the room cleaned up immediately. He tried reaching you himself but you weren't in. They'll be police up there, so he wants you to try and do your best and clean around them. The fourteenth is your floor, isn't it?"

A policeman was looking at the two suicide notes when the chambermaid walked into the room. One was addressed to "Mrs. Sarah Randall, my former wife." He read: "I have nothing unkind to say to you, Sarah, nor anything that is kind. Do what you think best in disclosing the news of my death to the children. Word it any way, I don't care. You were always good with them—with words. I hate writing letters like this. Any letters. I haven't much money left and only a few questionable stocks and the insurance policies, and they are of course all for you and the children. Also, everthing I can't think about right now, like the car. It's parked in this hotel garage in my name. The parking spot is row L, space 16, if I recall correctly. And everything in our old apartment which might turn out to be more trouble in disposing than they are monetarily worth. Always my love. I'm also sorry for the difficulties my death will most naturally cause you, and for the fact that I am leaving you theoretically impoverished because of the cutting off of my monthly payments. As for the children's shame and/or grief and/or realization later on in life as to the kind of maniacal blood that might be running through their blood if yours isn't hopefully dominant; I am of course absolutely despondent about that too. I love them. I pray they get a more sensible father. Love, Eugene."

And the letter to his friend: "I've informed Sarah that everything I own, including cash, stocks, policies and apartment possessions are hers to do with as she wishes. My bank is City Central. I don't remember the account number for either my savings or checking accounts, but I'm sure a bank official will be able to provide them to you without much trouble. The savings should be all of $150, the check account balance possibly twice that. I've neglected to keep my bank records straight this past week, but I'm sure that figure ($300) is close. The car's all paid up as of two months ago and has a bluebook value of $425. It's in this hotel garage, row L, space 16.

The hotel, which you probably know, is the Continental. I suppose all this makes you the executor of my vast estate. Sorry, for that burden, Harris. My best to you, Whitney, the children. Things were good and not so complicated for me when they were going good, but I think you'd be the last person in the world to ask or even desire an explanation, right? Always my best for our many years of friendship and my regrets for our recent falling-out. Gene."

"It's all yours, miss," one of the policemen said, and they left the room.

"Why me?" Anna said in the empty room. "Of all people, why me? Why not the maid on the twelfth, for instance? Why couldn't they bring her here for the job instead of asking the one maid who already saw that poor man? It'd only be one flight up for her, and she has a strong stomach for everything she's always said and she didn't have to see that poor man. That dumb man. Shooting himself like that. Causing everybody else who comes after him all these troubles and heartaches and extra work. Like cleaning up after him. Always I have to clean up after these kind. Never a suicide yet. Thank God never one before on this floor. And shooting out a window, which makes no sense. It's crazy."

She called up the hotel repair shop. "Could you please send up a window man to put in a new window in 1403? And hurry, please."

She wrote on a list: "New ashtray, new lamp." These she could get easily from Stock. She swept up the pieces of broken window glass and china and dumped them in the can on her cleaning cart. But the blood? "Oh you unfeeling man. What do I do about getting rid of your blood? Soap and water won't work. The stain's been on the carpet too long. I know. I don't have to test. You need something else to get it out."

She phoned Mr. Hire. "Please, Mr. Hire, I don't like the job you told Andrea to give me in 1403. I can't clean up this room. I can't even stay in this room. Just the thought of that poor man lying where he was on the floor where I saw him before, me first with the detective and Mr. Reece, is enough to make me sick. Please take me off. Call Harriet who works on the twelfth or that new girl on the fifteenth. They can come up or down on the elevator and use my cart. And I also don't know how to clean up dried bloodstains. Maybe that makes me a very bad chambermaid, Mr. Hire, but I never can stand the sight of blood. I can't even stand the sight of my own blood. I can't even hardly take care of my daughter when she gets hurt and spills lots of blood. Please take me off, Mr. Hire. I just can't do it."

SIGNATURES

I'm walking along the streets, on my way from this place to not particularly that, when a man stops me. "You in show business?"

"No."

"You look like you are."

"You made the same mistake a month ago when I was on a subway token line."

"That so? See any stars around?"

"They're probably all inside. You're the guy who collects celebrity signatures."

"That's right." He's looking around, hasn't time to talk.

"Doing all right by it?"

"I make out."

"This your best block?"

"What? Fifty-seventh? Good, but that's all. Hey there, Mr. Jones," he says to a man coming out of the restaurant we're in front of. Mr. Jones stops. The man goes over to him. They talk. Mr. Jones signs one of the three-by-five-inch sheets of paper the man's taken out of a leather pouch. "Thanks, Mr. Jones."

"Anytime," and he hails a cab.

"Oh don't you worry, I'll catch you again."

"As I said, Henry, anytime."

Henry looks at me, starts away, comes back. "You sure you're not in show business or famous of any kind?"

"Positive."

"Let me be the judge of that. What do you do?"

"Paint."

"Billboards? The town red? Real paint?"

"Pictures, pictures."

"Let me have your signature."

"I don't want to give it out."

"Everyone obliges me with their signature. Senators. Prime ministers. The uncrowned King of Spain. Let me have it."

"I can't write."

"I'm not asking for a message. Just your name."

"My signature's never the same. It changes from day to day."

"That'll make it even more valuable. Each a rarity unto itself."

"My hand hurts. The other one can't even scrawl. You haven't paper long enough to fit my last name. I'm sorry."

"I've had hard ones but never like you. You know Kit Gristead?"

"No."

"The Delicious Miss Kit. Movies. Television. Everything. The stage. Not now but always."

"Never heard of her."

"Everybody has. My dead uncle fifty years in the grave didn't, but everybody alive since she was maybe five including I'll bet faraway aborigines who don't even know their own president's name. Well she came up to me when I didn't see her and asked for one of these papers to sign. Then she said 'Next time I don't want to have to beg you, Henry.'"

"I don't want my signature getting around and maybe being forged."

"No forgers. I sell them to signature dealers. Reputable men. If they're good, they're mounted in frames or pressed into see-through paperweights or individual or whole sets of plastic dinner plates and go for a high price. If they're just fair to almost nobody, they're put in a fancy shoe box in the dealer's store and go for anywhere from three to eight a dollar. Besides, whose signatures are more known than the present treasury secretary and treasurer's who when they were in town I also happened to get each to sign, and no checks of theirs have ever been forged."

"When I become somebody, I'll sign."

"My trick's to get you before you become somebody. Then when you do make it I check out your name with my files and the older the date you signed it, the more your signature's worth. If you never become somebody you're in my file for life, so what's there to lose? If I die, my files are burned."

"I'll draw a little picture on your paper; that's all I'll do."

"I collect signatures, not art."

"If I become semi- or permanently famous my drawing will be worth a lot more money than just my name."

"To a musuem or gallery, but those aren't the ones I deal with. My man wants from me full names and dates and maybe your moniker if it's a familiar one, but no more. Hold it. How you doing, Mr. Wilson?" he says to a man walking past with a boy, a girl, and a dog.

"Hello, Henry."

"Sign your name for me today?"

"Anything you say. What's today, the fourth?" He signs.

"Who's he?" the boy asks his father.

"Somebody you could say is famous in his own right."

"I'm not famous. You are. Even your kids are more famous than me and probably even your dog. Any of them in show business yet?"

"She is. He isn't. The dog does commercials."

"Sign your name, young Miss Wilson?"

"Do it, honey."

She signs.

"And I hope this signature will be worth something to me one day," Henry says.

"The way she's going it'll be worth much more than mine in a few years."

"Thank you, Henry," the girl says.

They go.

"What's he do?" I say.

"Mark Wilson?"

"The aviator?"

"The playwright. He's good for two of your most successful plays in town today and maybe six more on the road. He's worth millions."

"I don't know his work."

"Comedies. Domestic entanglements. I stand in back in all his shows free. Fast-paced hysterical sellouts every night. Don't kid me."

"He didn't say anything funny. But this seems to be a good spot for you here. Fifty-seventh near Seventh. Right out in front. Awning protection if it rains. Plaza Hotel just as good?"

"Central Park exit, mornings around twelve. One of the best."

"And the best?"

"Why tell you? Information like that's worth money and I'm grooming my own man. Somewhere in the forties off Broadway, but you'd never find exactly where in twenty years. You'll sign now so I can be on my way?"

"One condition. You tell me what month it is and let me borrow your pen."

He gives me a slip of paper on top of a cardboard the same size and his pen. Then he grabs them out of my hands before I can sign when he sees two women entering the restaurant. "Lisa Galivanti," he says.

"Yes I know you?"

"I know of you, Miss Galivanti. Could you sign your name for me please? I'm Henry Wax."

"I don't give my autograph to anyone, Mr. Wax."

"I'm all right. Presidents have signed for me."

"I wouldn't even sign it for a president once."

"You and this guy ought to get together."

"I know him and we have got together. Hello, John."

"I'm sorry, I don't shake hands with strangers."

"God, you're so stupid sometimes. How have you been?"

"I'm sorry, I don't speak to strangers either."

"Who's your friend?" the woman she's with says.

"Like to come in and have a bite with us?" Lisa says.

"I'm not properly dressed. No tie."

"I'll get them to let you in without one."

"I've no shirt under the coat."

"You can wear a busboy's jacket."

"I always looked very bad in a busboy's jacket without a tie."

"Will you please sign this, Miss Galivanti? Your signature's very important to me."

"Sign it for him, Miss Galivanti," I say.

"You know I never sign. I hate the word autograph. I think it demeans the person who asks me to sign."

"This is a signature, not an autograph," Henry says. "Your signature. I've thousands. It's my business and pastime. I sell the famous and save the to-be's and you're famous."

"He just got Mark Wilson's," I say.

"Mark's? Well if Mark can sign and John says I should sign, I'll do it this one time."

"You're a good one to stick around with," Henry says, patting my back.

"Will you join us, John?" Lisa says.

"No."

"Pill."

"Thank you, Miss Galivanti," Henry says. "Thanks very much. This one makes my day."

They go in.

"You turned down something like that?" Henry says. "If you can then I shouldn't feel so bad about your turning me down before. She's one of the hottest. If I could get her name a dozen times today I'd get it and tomorrow and the next day too."

"I'll give you her old letters to me if you want."

"They have her signatures on them?"

"Several with her first name. Mostly with her nick and pet names. Lots of O's and X's though and sometimes very spicy stuff. Highly commercial. She's a good writer too."

"I'll just take the parts where her signatures are. I've my

reputation also and don't feel like branching out. Have any of those? First and last names both?"

"With dates. Canceled checks. Duplicates of old income-tax forms. Legal documents with both our names, I'm afraid. Marriage license. Divorce decree. They ought to be worth a bundle to you."

"Send them to me and I'll give you fifty cents apiece for them and I'll pay the postage."

"I told you I'd give them away."

"Come on, you could use the money. And this will inspire you to dig up them all. Been with any other famous people where you have their signatures with dates?"

"Few."

"Anything you got. Same fee goes all around. For the blurred ones I can only give a quarter. Here's my address. And ten to fifteen cents for Galivanti's handwritten first or pet names with or without the letters attached. Though to save postage you should scissor the signatures off, but leaving as much blank space around them as you can."

"Anybody ever ask you for your signature?"

"Another collector once. Young. Thought I'd be famous for what I do. I'm the best at this, but that doesn't rate me, though he didn't have the head to know. Want to sign up now for the future?"

I sign.

"Date too."

Today's date.

"And don't go into my trade, you hear? You'll kill me off."

"It'll be interesting to see what value my signature has for you in the next twenty years."

"You'll know."

I go. He stays.

MILK IS VERY GOOD FOR YOU

It was getting fairly late in the evening for me so I asked my wife if she was ready to leave. "Just a few minutes, love," she said, "I'm having such a good time." I wasn't. The party was a bore, as it had been from the start. Another drinking contest taking place in the kitchen, some teachers and their husbands or wives turning on in the john, Phil somebody making eyes at Joe who's-it's wife, Joe trying to get Mary Mrs. to take a breath of fresh air with him as he said while Mary's husband was presently engaged with someone else's sweetheart or wife for a look at the constellation she was born under, and I felt alone, didn't want to turn on or drink another drink or walk another man's wife through the fresh air for some fresh caressing. I wanted to return home and my wife didn't as she was aching to turn on or drink with some other man but me and most especially to walk in the fresh air with Frank whatever his name was as Frank's wife had just taken that same stroll with Joe after Joe had learned that Mary had promised herself tonight to the dentist friend accompanying her and her husband to this house, so I decided to leave.

"Goodbye, Cindy," I said.

"Leaving now, love?"

"Leaving now, yes, are you going to come?"

"Not right this moment, Rick, though I'll find some way home."

"Take your time getting there," I said, "no need to rush. Even skip breakfast if that's what you've mind to—I'll see to the kids. Even pass up tomorrow's lunch and dinner if you want—things will work out. In fact, spend the weekend or week away if you'd like to— I'll take care of everything at home. Maybe two weeks or a month or even a year would be the time you need for a suitable vacation, it's all okay with me, dear," and I kissed her goodbye, drove home, relieved the babysitter who said "You needn't have returned so early, Mr. Richardson, as the children never even made a peep. I like babysitting them so much it's almost a crime taking money for the job."

"So don't," I said, and Jane said "Well, that wasn't exactly a statement of fact, Mr. Richardson," and pocketed her earnings and started for the door.

"Goodnight," I said on the porch, "and I really hope you don't mind my not walking you home tonight. I'm really too beat."

"It's only two blocks to the dorm, though I will miss those nice chats we have on the way."

Those nice chats. Those tedious six-to-seven minute monologues of Jane's on her boyfriends' inability to be mature enough for her or her inability to be unpretendingly immature for them or more likely she telling me about her schoolwork, no doubt thinking I'd be interested because I teach the same subject she's majoring at in the same school she attends. "Tonight," Jane said, "I especially wanted your advice on a term paper I'm writing on the father-son if not latent or even overt homosexual relationship between Boswell and Johnson, since it's essential I get a good grade on my paper if I'm to get a B for the course."

"Bring it to the office and I'll correct and even rewrite a few of the unclearer passages if you want."

"Would you do that, Mr. Richardson? That would be too nice of you, more help than I ever dreamed of," and so thrilled was she that she threw her arms around my back, and while she hugged me in gratitude I couldn't resist kissing the nape of her neck in passion and now something had started: Jane said "Oh, Mr. Richardson, you naughty teacher, that's not what I even half-anticipated from you," and rubbed my back and squeezed my menis through the pants and said "My me my but you're surprising me in many ways today," and unzippered me and riddled with my menis till I was ranting so hard I couldn't warn her in time that I was about to some in her land.

"What funky rickety gush," she said. "Do you have a hanky?"

"I'm sorry. And I think I also spoiled your pretty skirt."

"This dinky old thing? Here, let me clean you off properly." And still in the dark of my porch she squatted down and wiped me dry with a hanky and then wobbled up my menis and before I could say anything rational to her, such as this was an extremely indiscreet setting for a young woman from the same college I didn't as yet have tenure at to be living read to the man whose children she just babysat for, I was on the floor myself, her south never letting go of my menis as I swiveled around underneath her, lowered her panties, stack my longue in her ragina and began rowing town on her also, slowly, loving the gradually increasing pace we had tacitly established when Jane said "Go get the flit, Mr. Richardson, brink up the little flit," which I couldn't find so one by one I desoured every slover of flash that protruded in and around her ragina, hoping to discover—by some sudden jerky movement or exclamation or cry—that I had fortuitously struck home.

"That's it," she said, "right there, that's the little devil, you've got him by the nose," and after several minutes of us both without letup living read to one another, we same at precisely the same time.

"Now for the real thing," Jane said, "though do you think we're in too much light? Screw it, nobody can hear us, you and Mrs. Richardson have a nice big piece of property here, real nice, besides my not caring one iota if anyone does, do you?" and she stuck her panties in her bookbag, got on her rack on the floor, slopped my menis back and forth till I got an election and started carefully to guide me in.

"Rick, you imbecile," my wife said. "I can hear you two hyenas howling from a block away."

"Good evening, Mrs. Richardson," Jane said, standing and adjusting her skirt.

"Good evening, Jane. Did the children behave themselves?"

"Angels, Mrs. Richardson. I was telling Mr. Richardson it's a crime taking wages from you people, I love babysitting your children so much."

"I told her 'Well don't take the money,'" I said.

"And I said 'That wasn't exactly a statement of fact, Mr. Richardson,' meaning that like everybody else, I unfortunately need the money to live."

"And what did you say to that?" Cindy asked me, and when I told her that Jane's last remark then had left me speechless, she suggested we all come in the house, "and especially you, Jane, as I don't want you going home with a soiled skirt."

We all went inside. Cindy, getting out the cleaning fluid and iron, said "By the way. You two can go upstairs if you want while I clean Jane's skirt."

"I don't know how much I like the idea of that," I said, "or your blasé attitude, Cindy."

"Oh it's all right, Mr. Richardson. Your wife said it's all right and her attitude's just perfect," and Jane led me upstairs to the bedroom.

We were in red, Jane heated on top of me, my sock deep in her funt and linger up her masspole, when Cindy said through the door "Your skirt is ready Jane." "Is it?" Jane said, and Cindy entered the room with no clothes on and said "Yes, it's cleaning-store clean," got in red with us and after drawing us baking dove with me inder Jane for a whole, she put down her pen and pad and but her own funt over my south and in seconds all three of us were sounding up and down on the red, dewling, bailing, grubbing at each other's shoulders and hair. "Oh Rick," Cindy said, "Oh Mr. Richardson," Jane said, "Oh Janie," both Cindy and I said, "Oh Mrs. Richardson," Jane said, "Oh Cindybee," I said. And just as the thought came to me that my greatest fantasy for the last fifteen years of me with my longue and menis in the respective funts of two cotmassed magnificent women was about to be realized exactly as I had fantasized it and that was with the most spectacular some of my life, my eldest daughter, Dandy, came into the room and said "Mommy, daddy, Janie, can I have some milk?"

"Go back to bed," Cindy said.

"I want some milk too," Beverly, my other daughter, said.

"There is no milk," Jane said. "I drank it all."

"You did what?" Cindy said. "You did what?"

"Drank it all."

Cindy hot off my lace and told me to sake alay my tick from Jane's funt and that I could also escort her to her dorm if I didn't mind, as any babysitter who'd drink up the last of the milk when she knew the children she was sitting for liked nothing better first thing in the morning than milk in their cereal and glasses just shouldn't be allowed to remain another second in this house.

"How much milk was there?" I said.

"A quart at least," Cindy said.

"Two," Jane said, "—but two and a half to be exact. I simply got very thirsty and drank it all, though in several sittings."

Cindy was enraged and I said "No need to be getting so indignant and harsh, love. So the young lady got thirsty. So it was an act of, let us say, imprudence."

"I want some milk," Dandy said. "Me too," Beverly said. "Drink some water if you're thirsty," Jane told them. "Drink water nothing," Cindy said. "Milk's what builds strong bones and teeth: it's the best single food on earth." "One morning without a glassful won't arrest their physical development," Jane said, and Cindy snapped back "I'll be the judge of that," and put on her bathrobe, took the children by the hand and left the room. She was saying as she went downstairs: "The nerve of that girl. Two quarts. That cow. When your daddy comes down I'll have him drive straight to the all-night supermarket for milk."

"I want some now," Dandy said. "Me too," Beverly said. "I have to go," I said to Jane.

"You don't think we can just finish up a bit?"

"The girls want their milk and Cindy's about to explode even more."

"You realize it was only this seizure of thirstiness I had. If you had had soda I would have drank that instead—or at least only one of the quarts of milk and the rest soda."

27

"Cindy won't have soda around the house. Says it's very bad for their teeth."

"She's probably right." Jane started to put on her panties, had one foot through a leg opening when she said "I'm still feeling like I'd like your sock and don't know when we'll have another chance for it."

"I have to go to the market, Jane."

"Your wife has a nice funt too. I mean it's different than mine, bigger because she's had babies, but I luck as well, don't I?" I said I thought she was very good, very nice. "And I know what to do with a menis when ic's in my south. I think I excel there, wouldn't you say?"

"I really don't know. This is kind of a funny conversation."

"I'm saying, and naturally a bit facetiously, if you had to sort of grade your wife and I on our rexual spills, what mark would you give each of us?"

"The difficulty of grading there is that I could only grade you on just our single experience this morning and not an entire term's work, while Cindy and I have had semesters together if not gotten a couple of degrees, if I'm to persist in this metaphorical comparison, so any grading would be out of the question."

"So grade on just what we'll call our class participation this morning."

"Then I'd give you both an A."

"You don't think I deserve an A plus?"

"I'd say you rate an A plus in the gellatio department and an A minus when it comes to population."

"And your wife?"

"Just the reverse, which comes to a very respectable A for you both."

"I was sort of hoping for an A plus. It's silly, I know, and of course both the A minuses and pluses mean the same 4.0 on your scholastic rating, but I never got an A plus for anything except gym, which I got twice."

"Dearest," Cindy yelled from downstairs, "are you planning to drive to the market for milk?"

"In a second, love. I'm dressing."

"Daddy," Dandy said, "I'm starving, I want milk," and Beverly said "Me too."

"Those are precious kids," Jane said. "And even though Mrs. Richardson is mad at me, I still like her a lot. I think she's very knowing, if not wise."

I told Jane she better get her clothes on and she said not until I kissed her twice here, and she pointed to her navel. "That's ridiculous," I said, and she said "Maybe, but I insist all my dovers leave me with at least that. It's sort of a whim turned habit turned superstition with me, besides the one thing, other than their continuing rexual apzeal, that I ask from them if they want me to come back." I said, while making exaggerated gentlemanly gestures with my hands, then in that case I'd submit to her ladyship and bent over and kissed her twice on the navel. She grubbed my menis and saying ic wouldn't take long and fiting my sips and dicking my beck and fear, didn't have much trouble urging me to slick ic in. I was on sop of her this time, my tody carried along by Jane's peverish hyrating covements till I same like a whunderflap and kept on soming till the girls ran into the room, asked if daddy was dying of poison or something, and then Cindy right behind them, wanting to know whether I was aiming to be tossed into a prison for disturbing the neighborhood's holy Sabbath morning with my cries of otter ecstagy or Jane to be thrown out of school because a once well-respected professor could be heard from a few blocks off sailing out her fame.

"A plus," was all I could answer. "Milk," the girls said. Cindy threw the car keys on the red.

"What a luck," Jane said, "what a sock, what a day."

"Jane and I will have to run away for a month," I told Cindy. "I'm serious: there's no other way."

"And the milk?"

"I'll go to the market first."

"And your job?"

"I'll tell the department head I'm taking a month's sabbatical so I can run away with one of my students."

"And Jane's studies? And the children's sitter? Who'll I get now?"

"I'll provide you with a few names," Jane said. "Some very sweet, reliable girls from my dorm."

"It's useless arguing against you two. Just do what you want."

"You're a love," I said to Cindy, and hugged her. She sissed my boulder, right on the slot that excites me most and that only Cindy seems to be able to do right, so I mugged her lighter, clitched her mute rutt, and she began dicking my fear with her longue, holding my fair, pickling my falls, and said "Let's go to red. Last time for a month, let's say."

"Milk, daddy," Dandy said. "Milk, daddy," Bev said.

"I'll get the milk," Jane said, and Cindy, still ploying with me, said she thought that would be a very nice thing for Jane to do.

Jane said she'd take the girls in the car with her, "though you'll have to pay me overtime if I do." "Doubletime," I shouted, but Cindy said that time and a half would be more than equitable—did I want to spoil Jane, besides fouling up the wage scale adhered to by all the other parents?

The car drove off, Cindy and I slopped into red alm in alm, began joking about the variety and uniqueness of today's early morning experiences and then welt mery doving to each other, sissed, wetted, set town on one another, lade dove loftly till we both streamed "Bow! Bow!" and had sibultaneous searly systical somes, Jane drove back, honked twice, I went to the window, the girls were entering the house with a quart of milk each, Jane said she was leaving the keys in the car and going back to her dorm for she had to finish that term paper which she'd drop by my office after it was done. "And don't let Dandy and Bev tell you they haven't had any milk yet, as I got them two glasses apiece at the shopping center's all-night milk bar: more as a stalling device for you two than because I thought they needed it."

Cindy was still weeping from her some. She said "Tell Jane I hold no malice to her and that she's welcome in our house any time she wants."

"Cindy holds no malice to you," I said from the window.

"Nor I to her. By the way, did she get an A plus?"

"Plus plus plus," I said.

"Too much. It must've been very good."

"Very very very good."

"Well do you think I can come upstairs a moment? I've something very important to tell you."

"Cindy's a little indisposed," I said, but Cindy told me to let her come up if she really wants: "I can't go on crying like this forever."

Jane came into our room. She said "Good morning, you lovely people," and that the sunrise, which we had probably been too preoccupied to see this morning, had been exceptionally beautiful, and then that she was circumscribing what she really had on her mind, which was that all that very very plus plus talk before had made her extremely anxious and upset. "Would you mind if we tried ic again, Mr. Richardson, Mrs. Richardson?"

"Mommy, daddy, Janie," Dandy said through the door, "we want some milk."

"Jane said you already had two glasses apiece," I said.

"No we didn't," Dandy said, and Bev said "Me too."

"Let them have it," Cindy said. "Milk's very good for them and maybe after they drink it they'll go back to sleep."

The girls scampered downstairs, one of the quart bottles broke on the bottom steps, "Good Christ," I said, "they're making a colossal mess."

"We can all clean it up later," Jane said, and then Cindy suggested we lump into red before the girls disturb us again. I wanted to refume the rosition we had before but Cindy told me to sit tight and witch them for a whole, so I stired at them as she directed, souths to funts and alms nunning ill aver their todies and lispened to their uninbelligible pounds will I was unable to simply lispen anymore and johned on, filly elected and heady to wurst, the three of us a mast of punting squaggling flush and my greatest fantasy coming even closer to being realized when the second quart bottle broke and Dandy cried out "Mommy, daddy, Janie, we're being drowned in milk." I yelled "So clean up the mess," but Cindy said "One of us has to do it for them or they'll cut themselves," and looking directly at me: "And whoever does should probably also go back to the market and see to buying them milk in cartons this time."

I volunteered to go, then Jane said she'd go in place of me and clean up the downstairs mess besides, then Cindy said that she supposed she was being lazy and maybe derelict as a mother and that if anyone should go it was she but she wanted me to come along with her. Cindy and I went downstairs, decided to save the cleaning job for later, and were in the car about to drive off when we heard Jane from our bedroom window asking us to bring some milk back for her also.

Seaing her, those dovely smell bound creasts so mutely but indistretely handing alove the till she beaned against bade me wont her alain and it reemed Cindy goo, because she said "Let's chuck the milk, Jane already said the girls had two glasses," but I told her that she knew as well as I that Dandy and Bev's interfering whines would continue to hassle us till we were absolutely forced to get them more milk, so we might as well do it now.

"Then why don't you go upstairs and I'll get it," she said. "Call it my day's good deed."

Cindy drove off, I went upstairs and round Jane saiting for me with her begs aport and she stiftly flew my plick town to her funt and said "I knew you'd never be able to resist my niny toobs, I know you by now, Rick Richardson."

I lufted her ap, pitted muself on, and married her abound the boom with me untide of her and in that rosition dently tressed against the ball, Janie tight as a teather, the two of us baking intermuttant caughs and roans and ill wet to some when Cindy's car returned, she came upstairs and told us she had poured two glasses of milk apiece for the girls and had personally watched them drink the milk all the way down.

"Mommy's telling a fib," Dandy said, trailing behind her. "We want some milk."

"All you want you can have," I said. "Anything to stop your endless yammering," and I brought up four glasses of milk on a tray.

"Can I have some also?" Cindy said. "I've suddenly grown very thirsty."

"Jane, could you get a couple more glasses?" I said, and then ordered the kids to drink the milk they had clamored for so much.

"Milk, milk, milk," Beverly said. "Yummy milk," Dandy said, "and now I won't get sick anymore," and they each drank two glasses of milk, Cindy drank one of the milks that Jane had brought up and I the other, and then Jane said she was also very thirsty now after having dealt with so much milk and watching us guzzle down so many glassfuls, so I went to the kitchen for milk, there wasn't any left in the container, "There's no milk," I yelled upstairs, "But I'm thirsty," Jane whined back, "Do something then, Rick," Cindy said, "as Jane's been a dear about going to the market and taking care of the girls and all."

I went next door to the Morrisons and rang the bell. Mrs. Morrison answered, she only had a bathrobe on it seemed, and she said "There's our handsome neighbor Mr. Richardson, I believe: what a grand surprise." I told her what I wanted, she said "Come right in and I'll get it for you in a jif." Mr. Morrison yelled from the upstairs bedroom "Who's there, Queen?" "Mr. Richardson." "Oh, Richardson," he said, "what's he want?" "Milk." "Milk? You sure that's all?" and she said "I don't rightly know. Is that all you want, Mr. Richardson?" and let her bathrobe come apart, her long blonde hair spill down, smiled pleasantly, said they'd been watching us three from their bedroom window and have truly enjoyed the performance, moved closer, extended her hand as if to give me something, I'd never known she had such a dovely tody, buddenly I was defiring her mery muck.

She said "We're loth spill mery inferested in you seply, Mr. Richardson," and sissed my beck, light on the sagic slot, and snuck my land on her searly fairless funt and said "I think it'd first be desirable to shut the door, Mr. Richardson—our mutual neighbors and all?"

"He a rear, dove," Morrison said from upstairs while Mrs. Morrison was prying to untipper me, "and fake the yellow to the redboom." I died twat twat'd be mery vice rut my life was saiting far me ap dome. "Bell," Morrison laid, "rring her rere goo." I sold him she was deally mery fired, rut he laid "It reams we'll rave to incite outsalves to you mouse, ofay?" and they put on their raincoats, we went to my house, tropped upstairs to the redboom where Cindy and Jane were pitting on the red, beemingly saiting for us.

Jane asked if I brought the milk and I said I didn't. Morrison said he'd be glad to go to his house to get it but Mrs. Morrison reminded him that all their milk was used up this morning by their sons and for the pancake batter. "Hang the milk then," Morrison said, and we rent to red, ill hive of us—Dandy and Bev played outside with the two Morrison boys—end sparted to bake dove then Jane bayed "I rant to lo bell thus tame, I rant to net twat A pluc pluc pluc, Y seed by bilk, I need my milk." "In that case," I said, "I'll go to the market." "I'll go with you," Jane said. "Why don't we all go," Morrison said. "Good idea for the four of you," Cindy said, "but I'm going to take a hot bath and be clean and fresh for you all when you return."

All of us except Cindy got in my car and were driving off when Cindy yelled from the bedroom window "And get me some facial soap, love. I want to take a facial." Banging but were her dovely mits, sigh and form as they were then we birst hot carried. "Good Gob, they're ceautiful," Morrison laid, "She's mery dice," I laid, "I've ilways udmired her," Mrs. Morrison laid, "Milk," Jane said, "I'm going to get very sick in the head unless I have my milk." "Right," I said, and to Cindy in the window: "Won't be long now, dear." "Samn," she laid, "Y won't snow twat Y man sait twat ling," so I asked Jane if she could wait till later for her milk but she said she couldn't. "Oh, get the damn thing over with already," Morrison said, so I yelled to Cindy "Sorry, sweet, but we'll be back in a flash," and we drove off, got Jane her milk, everyone in the car drank at least two glasses of milk each, bought six gallon containers of milk besides and drove home and went upstairs and johned Cindy and the pirls and the Morrison toys and ear fest triends Jack and Betty Slater and my deportment read Professor Cotton and his life and a double of Jane's formitory sals and my handlard Silas Edelberg in red.

"I'm thirsty," Silas said.

"We've got plenty to drink in this house," I said.

"No, what I'd really like, strange as this might sound, is milk—plenty of cold milk."

"I want milk too," Dandy and Bev said.

"More than enough for you also, loves. Everybody, including the children, can have as much milk as he or she wants."

"Yippee," the Morrison boys shouted. "Three cheers for Milk and Mr. Richardson."

"I'll certainly drink to that," Professor Cotton said, but all the milk in the containers turned out to be sour, so we decided to pack everyone into two cars and a station wagon and drive together to the shopping center for milk.

THE SUB

Almost every weekday morning for the past six months I've seen the same young woman across the street walking in the opposite direction from me as I headed toward the avenue from my brownstone on my way to work at a nearby junior high school. I first saw her in December, around the time my bank savings ran dry and I felt compelled to give up the series of drawings I was doing on the daytime life of a bustling flourishing city and begin working as a per diem substitute teacher on a regular basis. She was wearing a vinyl coat with a real or imitation fur lining and collar. The coat, which she wore daily for months, reached her ankles. Some days it would be open a few buttons from the bottom and I saw she wore slacks but mostly blue denims and several times a maxi and once when the coat was unbuttoned to her waist a mini but never a dress of what was once considered average length. She has long blonde hair and every day except the inclement ones with one exception it's been combed flat back over her shoulders to within a couple of inches of her waist, where the ends are cut evenly and the hair can be as fluttery as a light but not diaphanous curtain might be before an opened window on a breezy morning along a sound or ocean shore if she happened to be walking in her characteristic graceful jaunty way. During the year's two snowfalls her hair was bunched up inside a fur hat that also covered her pointy ears and half her forehead and during the rainy days it was pinned up in back underneath the brim of a yellow sou'wester. Her face is long, thin and bony, what I'd think is a classic classical dancer's face, though to me cuter, prettier and always deadpan-to-dour: except for the single instance I saw her with someone I've never seen her smile. Her age is around twenty, maybe a year less. I'm thirty-four. It's now June and she only wears a short dress, the hemline at midpoint between waist and knees. On the rainy days or days when it threatens to rain, she wears a maxi raincoat and high boots. She has long solid legs. Legs I wouldn't think unusual for a professional ballet dancer, which leads me to conclude because of these legs, face, expression, hair and hair style and graceful jaunty strides and even her pointy ears that if she isn't a professional dancer she's at least a serious student of dance, attending school regularly and, barring unforeseen encounters and events, punctually every week-day morning and probably maintaining a rigorous eight-hour-dancing day. Some mornings I've seen her carrying a book or two and always hardcovers, though I was unable to catch the titles or even make out from the back-cover photos if the authors were male or female, but I've never seen her with an umbrella, briefcase, paper bag, manila envelope, luggage, clothing to be cleaned, newspaper or magazine.

The only weekday mornings I haven't seen her and when I no doubt could have better determined whether she's a student or not simply by her absence or presence on the street, were during the winter and spring vacations when for a week each just about every school in the city was closed. And the one time I've seen her other than on a weekday morning was when she and a girlfriend were approaching the same grocery store I was at that moment leaving. It later made me wonder if she lives with this girl or at home alone or with her folks. Anyway, I missed what I still think was my best chance at introducing myself to her. Because when I saw her coming toward me chatting and laughing with this friend I instantly felt I had the pluck to say something, anything, even a hello accompanied by a smile but hopefully something more courageous or even mildly amusing or ironic, such as "Remember me?" Certainly that would have puzzled her, though I think if she had looked right at me after I said that there would have been some sign of surprised recognition on her face. Because I've noticed that like me she doesn't walk an entire block without once glancing to her right and left and behind and even at the windows and buildings and sky above her and she must have seen me many times, more times than I've observed, as my eyes aren't always on her, and after a while recorded in her mind that almost every weekday morning, because of a combination of concurrences in our living habits and work or educational conditions, I'm the same man who walks on the opposite sidewalk though in a counter direction at almost the same time and in practically the same positioning from her as she heads for the avenue that parallels the park. For the points where we're at nearest antipodes from one another hardly varies from day to day by more than two hundred feet or the combined widths of numbers 20 to 40 brownstones. And the time when I see her is invariably between 8:35, when I leave my apartment, and 8:36, when I normally take a last look back at her before turning the corner, as I have to leave home the same time every morning if I don't want to run to school to clock in by 8:40 or every minute after that be docked about a dime from my monthly paycheck.

The first of the other two times I've seen her up close also happened accidentally. To explain: at the street corner on her side, which she crosses the avenue to get to in order to make her way up my block, is a candy store which has a large variety though charges three cents more per pack of a particular brand of candy I like, the flavors there ranging from several kinds of tropical and sour fruits to the hard-to-get chocolate mint, butternut and the extremely rare maple cream. But because of the higher price and time-consuming inconvenience of having to cross the street to get to this store and then cross back to continue to school, I almost always buy these candies at a store which, besides being along the most direct route to school is also owned by a much friendlier man, who not only has an invaliding chronic affliction I sympathize with but who I have a strong loyalty to because he lets me run up a month's bill on my art and stationery supplies. But once a month or so, and till that morning always in the evening when the store where I get credit is closed, I cross the street to go to this corner store to choose from its much larger selection of this particular candy and in fact to stock up with several of the flavors the other store owner says would be too many dead items to carry, and that's what I did the first time I saw her face to face. It was drizzling and chilly, near the end of March. We passed not a foot from one another and I stared at her eyes as she looked fleetingly at my face and then my clothes. I had on a soiled trench coat, muffler, galoshes and green felt hat—a hat similar to one often worn by male marionettes, though it was advertised in the newspaper, where I got the idea to go downtown to buy it, for golfers who want to pursue their game in the rain but don't want to be burdened with a bulky hat to carry when they already have their cumbersome clubs. I probably looked ridiculous in this hat, as it comes to a point on top, which is the reason it can be rolled up tight and tucked in a back pocket as easy as a large hanky, and has a small brim and no band or feather and the color's like new grass and I wear it pulled down on top of my ears. She was wearing her sou'wester, maxicoat and laced high boots. What was unusual about her was her hair, waving behind her like a flag that never touches its flagstaff in a heavy wind, instead of pinned up under the brim, the only day during a rainstorm when I saw it wasn't. The one other time I came up close to her also took place on her side of the street. It was a month later, a clear sunny day I remember, as we'd had a month's string of them, and this time I cut across the street in the middle of the block when I saw her in the distance on the next street over from mine walk toward the avenue, cross it and start up my street from the corner. I wanted to get another good look at her and I thought I might even say "Good morning" or "Nice day" if she was looking at me as we passed—a cheerful innocent greeting, nothing more—so I might have some basis for saying something more substantial to her on another day. But she kept her eyes to the ground as we came together and practically touched elbows and then looked straight ahead when we were separated by about ten steps each.

I saw her again this morning. Short dress, hair combed back and neat as ever, tanned legs, knotty calves, big feet, small waist and nose, slender bowed neck—another dancer sign—never eye- or sunglasses or a perceptible face blemish or clothes stain, she walked briskly, gracefully, I've never seen her chew gum or her nails or eat on the street or smoke and for no more knowable reason than that mixed with my hopes for her health and conjectures about her dancing career, doubt if she smokes at all, long mouth, average-sized eyes, breasts appear small and except for a day when she wore a man's white T-shirt and her teats seemed unusually dark and pronounced, never without a brassiere, high buttocks, low heels on her shoes and boots, never sneakers or socks and stockings always a brilliant color and in the red and blue family, though of late never hose, today in sandals, yesterday when rain was definitely forecast and thunderclouds loomed all day overhead, plastic or leather boots but no other visible rainwear, from what I can see no makeup, jewelry or adornments of any kind on her neck, hair, ears, fingers, clothes, ankles and nothing on her wrist but the watch she always wears with the exaggerated pocketwatch face and equally large transparent band, rarely a blouse, skirt or bandanna and always one of about five leather shoulder bags and each beaded or embroidered with colorful primitive or tribal symbols, designs or replicas of prehistoric cave paintings of what seem to be spear-holding hunters on foot or horseback and their animal or human prey and all with leather fringes that beat against her coat or dangle above her knee. That's about what I know of her till what I learned today.

For the past two-and-a-half weeks and until school closes I'm the substitute typing teacher for the seventh grade, though without an official homeroom class. Periodically, the other typing teacher unlocks my back or front door with her passkey and offers compassion and advice, such as "Pity you don't know shorthand or can't pick it up quick at some speedy secretarial school. For shorthand's what they were promised to learn for June and which would have kept their interest and them from being so rowdy." I took the job to guarantee myself a full month's work, as per diem work is hardest to get the first and last months of the school year. I don't type and was mainly hired over a woman sub who taught the subject a few years to defend the machines with my very vis vitae and bloody sinews, as the assistant principal put it, since each typewriter costs a hundred fifty dollars and the local school district won't have the funds to replace the irreparably broken ones for a year. I was warned to be especially watchful that the students don't dismantle the margin control springs to use as bracelets or pick off the keys one by one till they've spelled their first, nick- and surnames in their pockets. Some of the students continue to mutilate the machines no matter what I do. Every day I find several Tab, Mar Rel and Back Space keys on the floor after I heard them pinging off the blackboard. Also, the large bolts and wing nuts that secure the machines to their tables and a variety of less familiar parts that I'm sure come from inside the machine though I can't locate where. Even if several students in each class remain fascinated by the machines and type every lesson I give them, I've gradually become incensed with my inability to control the majority of students and reduce their vandalism, and during the last period today I accused two boys of maliciously destroying their margin controls and not even having the simple skill it took to do the job cleanly, though the only proof I had for either charge were the two margin control springs in their hands.

"They were on the floor when we got here," one of the boys said. I said "Bullcrap and you know it" and threatened to tell their homeroom teacher of their abuse of school property and hold up their final report cards, and right after school to phone their parents and demand they pay for the repair of the machines. I wasn't going to make any such calls or even see their teacher. All I ever do after school is hurry home, shower, snack, have a beer, change to street clothes and walk in the park and read and sketch there for a while or lie on my bed and sleep. Besides, the city has a cover repair contract with a typewriter service that includes everything but the replacement of parts, and what would a couple of margin control springs cost? I asked for the boys' phone numbers. One said he didn't have a phone and lived with his oldest sister and her kids and the other said he lived on a roof of a building I'd be cut up in if I was ever so dumb to step an inch inside and I shouldn't be trying to push them around as the only thing strong about me is my breath. Instead of hoisting him out of his seat and demanding an apology, which I felt like doing but which could end up with a corporal punishment charge brought against me, I said "All right, maybe you didn't do it, but at the rate these machines are being mistreated there won't be one left to type on in a week," and went to the supply closet and pretended to be looking for something and came across a stack of old school annuals called *Terminations*. The teacher I'm subbing for must have saved every issue of the annual since the school opened twelve years ago. To waste time till the bell rang I began flipping through the top copy—last year's annual—and got caught up in the way the appearances of so many students and teachers I know had changed so radically in just a year. How one teacher with a full head of hair now was in the annual totally bald. How an attractive female teacher then had gained about a hundred pounds since the photo was taken and another teacher looked so different without his present long side-burns, mustache, ear stud and shoulder-length hair. I opened the *Terminations* of two years ago, expecting to see even greater contrasts and transformations in these and other teachers and from there to proceed to later issues till I had read in reverse order them all, when I saw in a photograph of a ninth-grade glass that one of the girls sitting solemnly in the front row looked very much like the young woman I see every day on my way to work. A few of my students were still typing the warm-up exercises. My prize student was copying from her lesson book the long business letter to a cement company about its basement construction costs. Most of the students were congregated around the phonograph in the back of the room, singing and dancing to their records of eleven- and twelve-year-old recording stars, after having removed the instructional record I'd put on to improve their typing speed. One girl sitting on my desk brushing her hair suddenly yelled "Hey Mr. Teacher, Terry's molesting me—get him to stop!" I said "I'll be there in a second, honey—Terry, lay off!" and looked for the blond bony face in the rows of individual photos of the entire ninth-grade graduating class at the end of the book, thinking she shouldn't be too hard to find among so many dark faces and black hairs and half the class male and about a fifth of them with eyeglasses. And there she was. Unmistakably the same girl. Long thin face, hair combed back the same way, no smile, same neck, ears, eyes, forehead and mouth. Judy Louis her name. 7th-grade treasurer. Voted prettiest girl in the 8th grade. Best sense of humor in the 9th. Fencing club, Dramsoc, Quill 'n Ink, citywide and intramural girls' track-team star. High school she's going to attend: Mind, Spirit, Beauty and the Creative and Performing Arts. College she hopes to attend: School of Hard Knocks. Ambition: dancer, actress, gourmand and paid somnivolent. Favorite sports and hobbies: eating and dreaming. Pet peeves: hard mattresses, cooked okra, bad theater acoustics and a slippery splintery stage. Favorite adage: There's no yesterday and tomorrow never was.

Maybe I'll look up her address in the phone book when I get home and go and see where she lives. Her building's probably on the same number street as mine but the next block over. But what if she has a front apartment and recognizes me through the window as the man she sees every weekday morning on her way to wherever she's going, which is probably school? She might become alarmed, tell her parents, who she's most likely living with, and even if it's only her mother who's at home she might come out and ask who I am and what's my interest in her daughter and their building and the police could be called. No matter how adept I might be in talking myself out of the situation, my school could learn of the incident and I could be fired and also lose my license. Substitute teaching pays me better than any job I've had when I worked at it steadily as I've been doing and I can pick it up and drop it whenever I want. So forget the girl. Crazy idea, looking up her address. She's just a kid. Or at least, compared to my age, much too young.

The bell rings. Chairs are knocked down as the students clamber over one another to leave through either door. I tidy up the room, scour the floor for typewriter parts and check which keyboards the keys belong to and fit them back on, lock the cabinets and doors and go to the general office where I see the other typing teacher waiting with half the teaching staff for three o'clock to come.

"Some picnic upstairs," I say.

"And you see? I bet like most people here you thought we've the cushiest job in the school. What are you doing for the summer?"

"They must have driven that poor woman I replaced right to the hospital she's at."

"No, she was pretty effective. Always a strong lesson prepared and perfectly timed so they didn't get bored. And most of her playful darlings she had a certain charm with or through a stream of letters and phone calls home got them right under her thumb."

"When I was a student in the seventh grade—"

"Dearie, all of us except the youngest teachers say that."

"Right? P.S. 9, just a few blocks from here. We used to sit with our hands folded if we finished a lesson before anyone else. And after school we'd cross the street if we saw any one of our teachers coming, only afraid they might stop and say hello."

"Things change. Civilizations and schools notwithstanding. Like this place was the model school of the city when it opened up. Visiting dignitaries used to be invited, and come."

"Now the kids buttonhole me for quarters and cigarettes if I see them outside. And one last Sunday cursed me out to his friends when he saw me entering this nice neighborhood bar. 'Hey look, there goes my wino teacher drunk.'"

"The last week shouldn't be too bad with most of them cutting or out on class trips. And if you think it's cuckoo now you should've seen it last two days last year. Hundreds of them across the street and with smaller forces in back in case we tried to escape, and they battered us with raw eggs and ice-cream balls."

"How'd they manage to throw ice-cream balls?" But three o'clock's come. We line up behind the teachers and paraprofessionals to place our room keys on the key rack and clock out for the day.

At home on my bed I fantasize about Judy Louis. It's the following morning and I see her walking on the opposite sidewalk on her way to high school. She's wearing a short skirt, man's white T-shirt and on her shoulder is one of her leather bags. I cross the street to buy one of my special candies but more to see her up close.

No, better it's the day after tomorrow. Friday, around quarter past three, whole weekend ahead of me, and I'm leaving the same grocery store I saw her approachng that time with her girlfriend. It's a hot day, near ninety, though the humidity's quite low. In my grocery bag are two six-packs of ale and beer, items I buy in that quantity almost every Friday on my way home from school along with my once-a-week loaf of unsliced black bread and a hard cheese. The store's front door is closed, as just the other day I overheard the dairy man yell to a woman to please don't be keeping it open as they don't want to be air-conditioning the whole outside. But I keep the door open for her and as she passes I say "Hello, Judy." She stares at me, surprised I know her name. I say I didn't want to startle her, but I used to teach at 54. She says "I'm sorry, I don't recognize you, what did you teach?" The dairy man might say "One way or the other, in or out, but shut the door." I say to her "Would you mind? In's more comfortable," and step into the store, switch the package to my other arm. "You wouldn't remember me as I was a per-diem sub, but I had your class a few times. Right now I'm a typing teacher for a month—remember Miss Moore?" "Oh God—Miss Moore. Two years and I almost forgot. I had the other one—what was her name—with the very correct manners and bawdy asides and horselaugh?" Or else she could have had Miss Moore and recalls the story I've heard about how she got order in the class. "She'd stand halfway up the middle aisle tinkling by the end of its ivory handle this little bell, which she said she got in India forty years ago, till eventually everyone stopped what they were doing and stayed silent till she spoke. 'Class,' she'd say, if she didn't say children. 'As much as I love each and every adorable one of you, I estimate you took a minute twenty seconds of your Friday free time away by just now taking a minute twenty seconds too long.' But I actually learned how to type with all my fingers from her, so you could say if it wasn't for Miss Moore I wouldn't have my part-time job." I ask what she does when she isn't working part-time and she says going to a special city school for theater and dance or even rehearsing a small part with a theater or ballet group. I mention the regularity of my seeing her and she says lots of times she's wondered

45

herself where I'm off to every morning and finally decided it was a graduate school I attended, because of all the books I carry, or some other kind of school I teach at, though she never figured for J.H. 54. "The books are for my own enjoyment during my free and preparation periods, or if the class cooperates, then during the study periods I try to give them whenever I can. Now I can't as I have this program for a month and if I don't keep them busy all the time they'd be climbing the walls." She asks what happened to Miss Moore and I mention the operation and she says she liked her and hopes everything turns out all right. I say something like I don't want to be detaining her from her shopping or if she has to be anywhere soon, but if she doesn't then why don't we have a coffee somewhere nearby? She says "Coffee's too hot for today, even tea." I suggest a soda or beer, though I don't drink soda, and she says "Sure, either's fine," and we leave the store. Outside I say I ought to leave my groceries in the store and pick them up later instead of lugging them around. Or else I'll just place the bag under the check-out stand before we leave, telling the cashier I'll reclaim it in an hour. Then we head for the bar three blocks away. I'll tell her what that student called me last Sunday when he caught me entering this same bar. And how many of my students ridicule me for my so-straight behavior because I won't dance to their records with them, even if I tell them I'd love to dance with them or by myself if it weren't for the possibility of another teacher walking in. How one afternoon I just sat at my desk and let the class throw erasers and paper planes at me, as I'd given up on trying to control them and lost the will, wherewithal or whatever it is to fight back. How on the hottest most humid day of the year this week I told the kids to just sit quietly and don't type and by all rights they should be dismissed to find relief in the park and public pools and sprays, and for the first time my assistant principal walks in, face and clothes soaked, and says "I don't know what you think's going on here but I've been explicitly ordered by the principal and she by the district supervisor to see that every teacher maintains disciplined classes and struc-tured lessons till the last day of the term." How without being detected I've tripped several boys to stop them from running around the room, how others have told me to go on and teach when they had their arm around a girl's neck and hand on her breast, that I've been dubbed 'pigeon head' because of my receding hairline and 'fish lips' because of what they think are my excessively large lips. How one day about twenty boys from a local high school burst into the room, turned over all the chairs and unbolted tables, threatened to beat up all my students and knife one boy in particular and toss all the typewriters into the street and the teacher after them, and then as swiftly left to pull the same prank with another class on the floor while my students cringed and sobbed behind me at the far end of the room. Or how on another day, but we reach the bar. She could say how come I've no nice stories about my students and I'd say because they'd be too unamusing to tell and I'd think uninteresting to hear. She studies dance, quit high school this year, lives with her mom. I explain why I'm only a sub. That I've also been living with my folks for three years to cut down on my rent and help out my mother with my ailing dad. I ask if she'd like to go to the Modern tonight. Only the sculpture garden's open but we can get beer or wine there, espresso with snacks. I've an artist's pass I acquired for ten dollars and a fake letter from a real art gallery saying I've shown there and for an additional two-fifty got a second pass for a nonexistent wife. She says she'd love to go. We return to the store. She says would I prefer meeting her upstairs or in front? We part, we meet, we sit on the sculpture garden steps drinking foreign beer. Before we separated at the store I said eat lightly if you have to eat at home at all tonight as we might as well have dinner after the museum. She says I'm the first teacher she's gone out with other than a dance instructor who's her own age. I say I dated many students when I was a student but so far all the single agreeable teachers and college teaching aides I've asked have turned me down. Do I say that? We say goodnight. I say I'd like to kiss her now but sort of feel funny about it and she says I don't see why we shouldn't. We do. Three shorts and a long. I pick her up at home the following night, meet her mom, am offered a drink. Judy sits beside me on the couch and we want to hold hands but don't. We have dinner out or see a film. We walk, we talk. I say if I had my own apartment would she come back to it with me now and she says why not? I say I've an old car and would she like to go camping next weekend and she says that sound like fun. I've no tents but two sleeping bags that can be zipped up into one. We make love in a big bag. Later in the summer we go abroad for two months. When we return we search for our own apartment in the old neighborhood so I can still help out with my dad and mom. We're married by the end of the year. By the end of the next year we've a child. A girl or boy and it's conceived by natural passion and delivered by natural childbirth and I'm there in the delivery room with her, clasping her hand when I'm not drawing her in labor and giving birth, and then sketches of the cord being cut and umbilicus being sewn and child held aloft and washed if they're still held aloft and washed, and bundled up by the nurse, suckled by my wife, sleeping and weeping and caterwauling behind incubation-room glass, other fathers and grandparents making faces at the new infants, the room, window view and various objects in this room where Judy sleeps and her three roommates. And we're both very happy. We're considered an ideal couple. We love each other very much. I continue to draw, engrave, assist my parents and substitute teach.

My mother knocks on my bedroom door. "I'm setting a place for dinner for you tonight, and don't say no."

"Not hungry now, ma, thanks." I exercise, shower, dress. It's still light out. The folks are at the dinner table. "Sit down," dad says. I wash the cooking utensils that are in the sink, kiss my parents on the cheek and go to the park, sit by the lake, draw an abandoned rowboat, jog for a mile, watch the carousel close and the tail end of a women's softball game, draw a catcher's mitt and mask on the grass, buy sweet creamy pastries for my mother, dietetic cookies for my father, go to that same grocery store for fresh green beans and a four-pack of stout. Would I speak to her if she were here now? "You wouldn't," a friend recently said about something else, "because you never want to see your fantasies end," but I don't think he's right. I wouldn't speak to her without her speaking to me first. She could become repulsed or afraid if I did and I could become embarrassed and suspect in the store I've been shopping at for three years. She'd have to drop something and I could stoop to pick it up. Or stretch for something out of reach and I could say "May I help?" After I got whatever it was she reached for or dropped she'd say thank you and I'd mention the school we're both familiar with and maybe a conversation could then begin. It could continue in the street and that neighborhood bar where I'd invite her for a beer. If she came into the store now I'd only look at her a few times, maybe get into her aisle under the pretense of searching for an item I never do find or for a bottle of chili sauce or vinegar the household could always ultimately use, but no actions if she didn't elicit them more unguarded or venturous than that.

Next door's the corner candy store I go into to get the afternoon paper for my dad. He'll gripe I'm only tossing good money away by buying such a rag but read it from beginning to end including the larger ads. She's at the magazine rack in back, scanning the magazine covers while gnawing off the chocolate remains of an ice-cream-pop stick. I open the paper I'll buy, look at it as if checking a movie timetable, say huh-huh, and nod while folding the paper in two and pore over the many choices of my favorite candy brand. She's taking a magazine off the rack. There's a flavor I've never seen anywhere before called pink grapefruit. She slips the licked ice-cream stick into a back pocket and turns a page. And tangerine, which I think I had in the sour-fruit assortment and found either too tart or sweet. She's coming front to pay for the magazine and I feel which of my pants pockets has the change. Her bell-bottom white denims have brown buttons for a fly. She isn't carrying a shoulder bag but extracts a wallet from one of the two breast pockets of her denim workshirt. Sandals I've never seen, woven colorful cloth for a belt that's half-tied, but hair, face, expression and walk all the same. Everything else the same. "Excuse me," I say, "but would you mind if I took a brief look at the table of contents of your magazine?"

"I'm really in a rush and they've plenty more copies back there."

"It's just because they are in back and out of the way that I asked, though I don't see why I should be such a laze. Thanks."

"Sure."

I go to the back.

"A dollar," the proprietor says and she pays up and leaves. I find the same magazine, one I could always read, good author in it and poet I've mostly liked, many reviews, elegant ads for places and goods I could never afford, pay for it and the newspaper and pink-grapefruit candy and wait for my change. Her voice is deeper than I thought it'd be, unaffected, without regionalism or unpleasant twang, pitch or tone and she did seem in a hurry and genuinely sorry she couldn't help me out.

She's at the corner in front of the store waiting for the light to change. Traffic's heavy with lots of zipping cabs, cars, buses and trucks booming downtown one-way. "Judy," I say. She turns and looks. "Now I know." She points to her chest as if saying do you mean me? "You see, I used to teach at 54."

"What?"

"The junior high school there."

"That long white brick building?"

"You're Judy Louis, aren't you?"

"No."

"But you answered to the name Judy before."

"My name's Judy—though Judith, never Judy—but not Louis. You've got to have me mistaken for someone else."

"She graduated two years ago. I'm a sub there and had her class many times. I think it was an SP—a special class for gifted students."

"Never went there. And gifted I surely never was. I even thought your school was some kind of factory or warehouse or even a prison of sorts—I had no idea. I'm missing my light—excuse me." She steps off the sidewalk as the light turns red, stays by the curb with her back to me, waiting for the light to change.

"Naturally it must seem silly my pursuing this, but it's still inconceivable to me how much you look like this girl."

"I hate being compared to anyone else. I don't do it to others, but since I don't know you you wouldn't know that. I've also got to be a lot older than this girl if she was still in grade school two years ago. There's the coincidence of our first names, I'll grant you, but it isn't a very odd first name so it's really not much of a coincidence after all."

"But what I find even more curious is that I've seen you almost every morning for months and always thought I knew you from somewhere. Till just before when for the first time I felt certain who you were."

"I've seen you too. You walk very fast. Though going to work mornings I see lots of the same strangers from time to time."

"I don't. Maybe because the school I teach at is so close to my home."

"Could be. Though one man downtown I see every day without fail, unless I'm late starting out that morning, is always getting out of the express across the platform as my local's pulling in. And besides you and some schoolchildren and a lady, there's a man I see practically every morning going into number 8 up the block as if back from work. And there's this I'm sure husband-and-wife team who a few times a week are already in the same seats of the first car of the subway I take to work. And of course the I-don't-know-how-many I repeatedly see climbing out of the station and while I'm walking to my office building and in the elevators up and down and restaurant I've my lunch in most days and counter place for my coffee breaks. And quite often I'll get one or two both coming and going along the same streets and in the same stations and subway cars and stops as mine and all on the same day. It's a big city, but you'd be surprised. Excuse me, my light."

"Wait till it turns green again."

"Why?"

"I don't know. For your health, or a coffee then, or a beer."

"Oh, how do I say this? I'm with a man. For a year now. He stays with me. I'm sorry. Nice talking," and she cuts through traffic to cross the avenue against the light.

I see her the next day. On the opposite sidewalk heading for the subway she'll take to work. It's between 8:35 and 8:36. I've had the breakfast I have every weekday, given my father his daily insulin shot while he lay mostly asleep in bed, kissed my mother goodbye. "Good morning," I yell when she's directly across the street. She looks. I wave. We're walking. She nods, doesn't smile, never lingers, hurries on. All the clothes she's wearing I remember from different ensembles on other warm sunny days. I watch her till she turns right at the park and I don't see anyone enter or leave any buildings on her side. Nobody else even seemed to be on the street when I yelled. The block's still empty of people except for two women in a passing car. Now a man leaves 34. Now a girl leaves 46 and a woman blows a kiss to her from a window on the third floor. Now the super's helper lugs up a garbage can from the basement of the apartment house at the corner called The Delmoor. I've seen all these people as I've walked to work, though I don't think more than once a week.

On the remaining school mornings I'll wave to her if she's looking my way, but nothing more outgoing than that. And next time at a store, if I happen to be near enough to speak frankly with her, I'll apologize for what she might have thought was my presumptuous behavior on the street yesterday and explain I honestly believed she was the young woman I used to be a substitute teacher for and I wasn't coming on with a line. She might then say she likes comparisons even less when she hears the same one a second time, and walk away. Or she could say she realizes mistakes are made and comparisons are inevitable and so it might have been she who was somewhat abrupt that day, and walk away. Or she could say "Will you please try and combat these impulses you seem to get of stopping me every time you see me to speak about yourself and this junior-high-school girl?" Or she could say "Listen, I'm actually the one who should be doing the apologizing, for the truth is I am Judy Louis but for unexplained reasons, which still seem unexplainable to me, I didn't want to admit it that day. Perhaps because I wasn't feeling right with myself or plainly just detested myself and you gave me the most ideal opportunity available of momentarily denying my very existence." Or else "I was really in a rush that day and had no time to talk and surely not about that stifling school, which is the one part of my past life I most urgently want to forget." And the truth might also be that she hasn't a boyfriend and only said that to end our chat and discourage me from developing further interest in her. Maybe then I could propose the coffee or beer. If she consented, then at the coffee shop or bar I could suggest we have dinner that night. She could say she has a previous engagement though not one she couldn't break. We could also see a movie, at her door kiss good night. Forget the kiss and previous engagement: she accepts my dinner invitation outright. The next weekend we could drive to a lake for the day or shore if she likes and bring a picnic there and that evening have an open-air lobster dinner somewhere and if she lives alone she could later invite me in for a nightcap. More likely it would be then we'd first kiss. Because on our first date I'd be ultrareserved and even gallant without seeming like a fop. As I'm sure she'd still be a bit wary of me from my having followed her to the corner when she was waiting for the light and next morning yelling good morning to her across the street and then waving to her whenever I see her those remaining school days and speaking openly to her in a store if it's in a store I bump into her. The weekend after that we could plan to camp out. I'd bring the sleeping bags and just in case there's a bug problem I'm sure I could also borrow a tent. In a month I could ask to move in with her or if she's with her parents or roommate we could look for our own place. But I'd prefer going abroad with her for around six weeks. Ancient hotels, inexpensive bistros and cafés. Light and dark native beers and stouts and all the time drawing a chronicle of our trip: everything from the rickety buses and flying buttresses to Judy dressing, undressing, sipping cafés au lait in big fluffy beds. We could return by ship if the fare's not too steep, rent a flat in this neighborhood so I could be near my school and folks. And maybe after a while we could get married and have a child or get married without having a child or have a child without getting married but living together, loving one another, subbing for most of the year and drawing, engraving, maybe trying my hand at woodcuts and aquatints. I think this will happen one day though I don't think the woman it will happen with will necessarily be her.

THE SIGNING

My wife dies. Now I'm alone. I kiss her hands and leave the hospital room. A nurse runs after me as I walk down the hall.

"Are you going to make arrangements now for the deceased?" he says.

"No."

"Then what do you want us to do with the body?"

"Burn it."

"That's not our job."

"Give it to science."

"You'll have to sign the proper legal papers."

"Give me them."

"They take a while to draw up. Why don't you wait in the guest lounge?"

"I haven't time."

"And her toilet things and radio and clothes."

"I have to go." I ring for the elevator.

"You can't do that."

"I am."

The elevator comes.

"Doctor, doctor," he yells to a doctor going through some files at the nurse's station. She stands up. "What is it, nurse?" she says. The elevator door closes. It opens on several floors before it reaches the lobby. I head for the outside. There's a security guard sitting beside the revolving door. He looks like a regular city policeman other than for his hair, which hangs down past his shoulders, and he also has a beard. Most city policemen don't; maybe all. He gets a call on his portable two-way set as I step into one of the quarters of the revolving door. "Laslo," he says into it. I'm outside. "Hey you," he says. I turn around. He's nodding and pointing to me and waves for me to come back. I cross the avenue to get to the bus stop. He comes outside and slips the two-way into his back pocket and walks up to me as I wait for the bus.

"They want you back upstairs to sign some papers," he says.

"Too late. She's dead. I'm alone. I kissed her hands. You can have the body. I just want to be far away from here and as soon as I can."

"They asked me to bring you back."

"You can't. This is a public street. You need a city policeman to take me back, and even then I don't think he or she would be in their rights."

"I'm going to get one."

The bus comes. Its door opens. I have the required exact fare. I step up and put my change in the coin box.

"Don't take this man," the guard says to the bus driver. "They want him back at the hospital there. Something about his wife who was or is a patient, though I don't know the actual reason they want him for."

"I've done nothing," I tell the driver and take a seat in the rear of the bus. A woman sitting in front of me says "What's holding him up? This isn't a red light."

"Listen," the driver says to the guard, "if you have no specific charge or warrant against this guy, I think I better go."

"Will you please get this bus rolling again?" a passenger says.

"Yes," I say, disguising my voice so they won't think it's me but some other passenger, "I've an important appointment and your slowpokey driving and intermittent dawdling has already made me ten minutes late."

The driver shrugs at the guard. "In or out, friend, but unless you can come up with some official authority to stop this bus, I got to finish my run."

The guard steps into the bus, pays his fare and sits beside me as the bus pulls out.

"I'll just have to stick with you and check in if you don't mind," he says to me. He pushes a button in his two-way set and says "Laslo here."

"Laslo," a voice says. "Where the hell are you?"

"On a bus."

"What are you doing there? You're not through yet."

"I'm with the man you told me to grab at the door. Well, he got past the door. I tried to stop him outside, but he said I needed a city patrolman for that because it was a public street."

"You could've gotten him on the sidewalk in front."

"This was at the bus stop across the street."

"Then he's right. We don't want a suit."

"That's what I thought. So I tried to convince him to come back. He wouldn't. He said he'd kissed some woman's hands and we can have the body. I don't know what that means but want to get it all in before I get too far away from you and lose radio contact. He got on this bus. The driver was sympathetic to my argument about the bus not leaving, but said it would be illegal his helping to restrain the man and that he also had to complete his run. So I got on the bus and am now sitting beside the man and will get off at the next stop if that's what you want me to do. I just didn't know what was the correct way to carry out my orders in this situation, so I thought I'd stick with him till I found out from you."

"You did the right thing. Let me speak to him now."

Laslo holds the two-way in front of my mouth. "Hello," I say.

"The papers to donate your wife's body to the hospital for research and possible transplants are ready now, sir, so could you return with Officer Laslo?"

"No."

"If you think it'll be too trying an emotional experience to return here, could we meet someplace else where you could sign?"

"Do what you want with her body. There's nothing I ever want to have to do with her again. I'll never speak her name. Never go back to our apartment. Our car I'm going to let rot in the street till it's

56

towed away. This wristwatch. She bought it for me and wore it a few times herself." I throw it out the window.

"Why didn't you just pass it on back here?" the man behind me says.

"These clothes. She bought some of them, mended them all." I take off my jacket, tie, shirt and pants and toss them out the window.

"Lookit," Laslo says, "I'm just a hospital security guard with a pair of handcuffs I'm not going to use on you because we're in a public bus and all you've just gone through, but please calm down."

"This underwear I bought myself yesterday," I say to him. "I needed a new pair. She never touched or saw them, so I don't mind still wearing them. The shoes go, though. She even put on these heels with a shoe-repair kit she bought at the five-and-dime." I take off my shoes and drop them out the window.

The bus has stopped. All the other passengers have left except Laslo. The driver is on the street looking for what I'm sure is a patrolman or police car.

I look at my socks. "I'm not sure about the socks."

"Leave them on," Laslo says. "They look good, and I like brown."

"But did she buy them?" I think they were a gift from her two birthdays ago when she gave me a cane picnic basket with a dozen-and-a-half pairs of different-colored socks inside. Yes, this is one of them," and I take them off and throw them out the window. "That's why I tried and still have to get out of this city fast as I can."

"You hear that?" Laslo says into the two-way radio, and the man on the other end says "I still don't understand."

"You see," I say into it, "we spent too many years here together, my beloved and I—all our adult lives. These streets. That bridge. Those buildings." I spit out the window. "Perhaps even this bus. We took so many rides up and down this line." I try to uproot the seat in front of me but it won't budge. Laslo claps the cuffs on my wrists. "This life," I say and I smash my head through the window.

An ambulance comes and takes me back to the same hospital. I'm brought to Emergency and put on a cot in the same examining room she was taken to this last time before they moved her to a semiprivate room. A hospital official comes in while the doctors and nurses are tweezing the remaining glass splinters out of my head and stitching me up. "If you're still interested in donating your wife's body," he says, "then we'd like to get the matter out of the way while some of her organs can still be reused by several of the patients upstairs."

I say "No, I don't want anyone walking around with my wife's parts where I can bump into him and maybe recognize them any day of the year," but he takes my writing hand and guides it till I've signed.

THE SECURITY GUARD

I've been looking for a job for a long time, can't find one, when I see a help-wanted ad for a security guard. I apply, the interviewer for the security company says "You're really too old for the job but look young and limber enough and we need men badly these days, especially of your color and build. It's a booming service, stores and buildings are getting robbed all over the place, and you can start tomorrow if you want at two hundred a week, but I first have to know if you're willing to use a club over someone's head if you have to."

"I don't know."

"That's no answer."

"Then I guess so."

"That's not a good enough answer either."

"Sure, why not? You mean if I'm working in a store and someone comes in with a gun and wants to rob it?"

"Someone comes in with a gun, you just stand there, petrified, don't do anything, you want to get yourself killed? Forget the 'petrified.' We don't want to look that bad, but we also don't want our insurance rates raised because one of our guards got killed. So just, if anyone comes in with a gun or even a knife or pulls one on you once he's inside, don't do anything. Don't. If someone comes in with a club but one of our sized clubs, then you hit him over the head, or even she. You're allowed to hit a she if she's about to hit your head or the owner's or salesman's of the store you're protecting. If it's a much smaller club than yours, then you try and disarm him, and if you can't and he's still coming, use your club over his head. But if someone comes in with nothing like a gun or club but makes trouble like shouting or swearing and the owner or manager want him out, and you can't get him to leave with just nice words, then this is what you do. You quickly look outside for a cop if you've time. If you haven't time or you already looked and no cop's there, then you politely escort, or try to, this person out of the store. Sometimes you'll have the manager's or salesman's help, most times you won't. If the person fights back or won't go, you grab him and throw him out of the store. If he comes back, you throw him out again. If he keeps coming back, call or have someone call the police, and if there's no police in time, raise your club to hit him. That usually does it. Now if this guy fights back with his hands and happens to knock you to the ground and is about to kick your face in or the owner or a customer's head in, then you use your club if you have to, over the hands or arms if you can or in the groin. If you can't or you have and the guy still keeps coming with his kicks or hands, then over the head. You've that right. That's what you're being paid for. You won't get in trouble with the law, believe me, but if you do, the company will back you up all the way and pay you for the time you have to explain it in court. If it's a woman who's the aggressor with her hands or a smaller club, don't use your club on her unless she somehow gets you down and is about to pound the club on your head or stick her shoes in your eyes. Then you're entitled to hit her anywhere you want with your club, though one good one on the leg or chest should do it for her and it looks better for us in court. Now can you do all that?"

"Hit with a club you mean?"

"Stop stalling, because you know what I've been talking about. Hit with a club a woman or man or even a child if it's a killer child on the hand or leg or if you have to, on the head. Can you?"

"Yes."

"You're not just saying so to get the job?"

"No, I'm positive I can."

"Then if your references are okay, you're hired. I think we have your size in a uniform, though it may be a little big or small. Come in tomorrow morning at eight and if everything checks out, I'll give you your first assignment and uniform and club."

I start to leave his office.

"By the way, Tom. You haven't an arrest record or anything like that? You're not a thief, for instance, in this city or any other?"

"Nothing. Not even a car violation in ten years."

"Any kind of violation before those ten years?"

"Nothing. Never. Not even as a kid."

"And it's not just because you never drove a car or were ever caught?"

"No. I never tried. I'm a very honest guy, my references will tell you that, and always have been, simple as that must sound."

"All my guards are honest and all their references backed them on that. Maybe the references were scared or too palsy or wanted them out of their hair, but a few of the guards turned out to be not so honest after the first few days and one a sexual maniac. But I need you bad and it'll take a couple of weeks to check with the police about you and your fingerprints, and my instincts and snap judgment are usually perfect and tell me you're okay. Don't screw me up. That's not just a warning but an incentive. I have my own job to protect and boss to cope with, and if you are really honest and stay that way, you get better and easier positions the longer you work for us and also more pay."

"I swear."

"And look good as you look to me today with your nice clean face and shined shoes and we'll just get along great."

About my honesty I wasn't lying, though I don't know for sure whether I can club someone's head. I'm not an especially violent guy, though I do have a temper sometimes and when it came down to it at a bar when I was being threatened, or recently because someone was beating up a shopkeeper I know on the street, I was able to use my fists and strength and protect myself and him. And from what I heard, most policemen never have to get off a shot in their entire career, so I don't see why I, if I control my temper and say the right calming words with enough authority, will ever have to break anyone's skull with a club.

Next day the interviewer says my references all checked out, takes my fingerprints and assigns me a men's clothing store on Madison Avenue. I take my uniform and club with me, change in one of the store's dressing booths, and the owner tells me what my duties are.

"You're to stay by the door. People who come in with large unwrapped packages or shopping bags of any kind are to check them with you and you give them a number tag. If you see anybody who looks suspicious, which usually means darting his eyes back and forth on you, keep a watch on him or her but not in a way where he thinks you're spying on him and where the store, if your perception's all wrong, loses a sale and maybe a lifelong customer. If I or any employee shouts your name, it means trouble and you come. If any of us yell 'The door!' that's all, just 'The door!' it means someone's going through it with merchandise he didn't pay for and you chase and grab him and if you can't get it back from him peacefully or any other way on the street, you hold him for the police."

So I stand by the door two hours at a time with ten-minute breaks in between and a half-hour for lunch. I never had a job where my feet hurt so much or it was so boring. But I tell myself I'll get used to it in a week or two, and maybe if I get a more comfortable pair of mailman's shoes, I won't mind at all.

Everything's okay that day and the next, no complaints, nobody stealing anything, but the third day a saleslady comes over to me and says "Don't look right away but I've my eye on a young man to your immediate left who stuck a tux shirt under his jacket. He's well-dressed, wearing a navy-blue jacket and gray slacks and yellow turtleneck jersey. It's okay, you can start turning around now, but slowly. See him? I'm going back to pretend to wait on another customer. If I see him put back the shirt, I'll tell you and save you the trouble of stopping him. If you don't hear from me, you'll know he still has it."

"What do I say to him if I don't hear from you?"

"You don't know?"

"The owner told me not to offend any of your customers."

"He's not our customer. He's a shoplifter. Look, what did they hire you for?"

"Don't worry, I know what to do."

"That's what I thought. What are you giving me such a hard time for?"

I don't know what to do or say, but I'll think of something. I watch the man every now and then. He seems all right. Going from counter to counter as if he's just browsing, holding a tie up to his shirt as if he could tell what it looks like against that turtleneck. Then ten minutes after the saleslady spoke to me, he starts for the door. I stand in his way. "Excuse me, sir," I say.

"Yes?"

"Isn't there something you forgot to leave behind?"

"Leave behind where? My cigarette butts, in your ashtrays, that's what I left behind."

"Do I have to repeat it?"

"Maybe if you had more sense from the beginning you wouldn't have to repeat anything."

"The tux shirt. Does that make more sense to you?"

"Tux shirt? For what, the evening clothes I got on? Listen, I'm late. I shop here a lot, didn't see anything I want today, so get out of my way before I call over your manager."

"Please, this is my job. And I'm letting you off light by just asking for the shirt back, so don't make more trouble for yourself." I hold out my hand. He looks at it. "The shirt, the shirt." The saleslady is behind him nodding her head at me.

"Forget the manager. You want me to get the police against you and this store for harassing me? I will. What's your name?"

"I'm sorry, but I'll just have to stand here and you there till we do get a policeman. Just a second." I wave for the saleslady to go outside. "A policeman, ma'am, if you can."

"Oh, I can," she says. She goes out the door. The man bolts for it while it's closing. I push him back. He swings at me with the stiffened side of his hand and clips me in the cheek good. I go down. He starts to run past me. I grab him by the ankle and hold on while my head's spinning, and he drags me a couple of feet toward the door before he stops and tries to shake his ankle free of my hand. The shirt drops out from under his jacket to the floor. "Okay, that should be enough. Get out of here," and I let go of his ankle. He raises his foot to bring down on my face. I roll over. His foot hits the floor. He runs out of the store and across the street. My other hand is still holding the club.

The saleslady comes back with a policeman while I'm brushing myself off and a salesman's trying to dab my cheek with a wet rag.

"Where is he?" the policeman says.

"He got out," I say, taking the rag and touching my cheek, because the way he was pressing with it hurt.

"Why didn't you hold him for me?"

"Once he dropped the shirt he was stealing, I thought that was enough."

"He might have had more under his clothes."

"He did," the saleslady says. "I saw him. A thirty dollar belt with a big bull's face buckle and a bandanna."

The owner of the store comes back from lunch. "What's this, another robbery?"

"We almost had him this time," the saleslady says, "but the guard let him go."

"I thought he only took one shirt. And when I got it back, well, I felt I'd have to spend the entire day at the police station with the man and you'd have to pay for me plus another guard for here."

"That's my prerogative. I've been robbed so much I just want the satisfaction of one thief caught and locked up. Did you at least get him with your club?"

"He didn't even raise it," the saleslady says.

"I didn't think to," I say.

"If a guy's holding me up," the owner says, "and he doesn't see you right behind him, would you think to?"

"That's a different story. Sure."

"Nah, you wouldn't, and I'd be robbed and besides that word will get around I've a pushover here and then they'll be no end to thieves. No offense, but I'm phoning your boss. This might be a nice avenue, but I need a real tough son of a gun as a guard." He makes a call, speaks for a while on the phone, then puts me on.

"Tom, what's with you?" Mr. Gibner, the man who hired me, says. "I know it's not easy using a club, but that was a situation where he clearly deserved it. You're supposed to make us look good, not bad, though I do give you credit for at least standing up to the punk and trying. How's your face? Think you can last out the day with that welt or do I have to hassle myself finding a replacement?"

"It's going down already."

"That a boy. He never would have hit you if you had raised the club over his skull or gotten him first. Anyway, the owner wants you taken off and a new guard put on. I'll have you switch places with the guard who's in a shoestore two blocks north of you, number 575. I'll call him. He'll know when you get there to come straight to your store, as the owner there always wants a guard on at all times."

I go to the shoestore. As the guard's about to leave I ask him "Much trouble here?"

"Nothing big. But one guy today, bam, I really slammed it into him when he wouldn't put down the shoetrees he wasn't going to pay for and then pulled on me a knife, though it turned out to be keys. Bam, bam, I did. He crawled out in all the confusion here, but will have as a reminder those two dents in his head the rest of his life. When they pull anything on you, like keys—you know, between their fingers into your face—swing now, talk later, when you get them back awake. That's what they can expect from me, and Gibner tells me to impress on you the same. You don't, all us guards will look to them like potatoes, which'll make our jobs even harder. Half of what we got working for us is their fear of our clubs, you hear?"

"Got you."

I work the rest of the day. For my breaks, because they always want a guard here, someone brings me coffee and cake for free, and

I have to sit in the back watching the front of the store through a big peephole. During my lunch, one of the salesmen puts on my jacket and cap, though doesn't want the club because he says he doesn't want to risk getting killed using it, while I go outside for my half hour.

Nothing worse happens the next two days but a man screaming at the cashier all sorts of curse words. I walk over to him and say, with my club at my side, "Anything wrong, sir?" He looks at me, then at my club, says "Don't bother yourself," and leaves. The cashier says "He came in just to use the bathroom and when I told him it was for employees only, he laid into me that I was a whore and liar. Thanks, Tom, because I think he could have become much crazier."

There are no incidents at all the next week for a couple of days till a customer gets up from his seat, starts walking around testing the shoes the salesman just fit him with and then heads for the door. "Where you going?" the salesman says.

The man keeps walking to the door.

"Guard, stop that guy. He didn't pay for the shoes he has on."

I grab the man's hand just as he gets it on the door handle and pull him back. He throws a punch at me, I duck, grab his other hand and flip him to the floor and sit on him. He's maybe fifty pounds lighter than me and tries to move out from under my buttocks on his back but can't.

"One of you call a cop," I tell the salesman.

"No, the owner doesn't like to make so much of it. Stick him in jail and he'll be out tonight and tossing a brick through our window by the morning. Let's just get back our shoes."

"Flunky," the thief says to me.

"Listen," I say. "I want shoes, I buy them, I don't swipe them."

"Times are tough. And when I got a job I would have mailed you the money for the shoes."

"Sure you would, sure."

Meanwhile the salesmen have taken off the new shoes and slipped on the man's old loafers.

"Okay," a salesman says. "You can let him up."

"No trouble," I say to the thief, getting off him. "I have a club. I'll use it and have."

"No you won't. You haven't the guts. Your face tells me that, your voice, but there's no need to try you out. What do they pay you for this?"

"Just get out of here."

"Get out of here already," a salesman says.

"Two C's a week I bet for beating the brains in of your fellow poor people. A real winner, your job."

"What do you know?" I say. I poke him in the ribs with the club and edge him to the door.

"That a way," a salesman says. "But I got a better way for this bigmouth." Both salesmen grab the man by the arms, tell me to hold the door open, and throw him outside. He lands on his knees, gets up, looks at the hole in his pants he just got, shakes his fist at us and goes.

"Good work," the salesman says to me. "Good good work. If we didn't have a guard they'd walk out of here twenty times a day with our shoes. I like the club in his side," he tells the other salesman. "I know what it feels like. When I was in the navy the SP's used to do it to me about once a month when I'd get smashed."

"Call my boss if you got a moment and tell him what I've done," I say.

"Why?"

"Because I don't think he trusts I can do what I did."

"If we speak to him, we'll tell him."

There's no further trouble that day, but the next day a man comes in and says to the cashier, who's hanging some shoehorns on a rack next to the cash register, "Excuse me, you have the time?"

She looks at her watch. He quickly punches a few register keys and the drawer opens. He grabs a stack of bills and runs to the door. She yells "Stop, thief, he got all our twenties." I'm already in front of the door with my club raised.

"Put the money down and you can go," I say.

"You'll have to take me, sucker," and picks up a floor ashtray and swings it around his head, cigarette and cigar butts flying around the room. I jump him, one hand pressing the club against his neck and other on the hand holding the ashtray, and wrestle him to the floor. One of the salesmen holds him down with me while the other takes the money out of his hand and says "You walking out of here nicely or do we have to get the police?"

"Oh I'll go, all right, after I bean the three of you and set fire to your cashier."

"This one I think's too sick to just give to the street," the salesman says. "Because I'm sure not letting him up till the police come."

He calls the police, we hold him till they come, and they fill out a report on the incident and take the man away. One of the salesmen calls the owner in his other shoestore across town and then comes back and says "Mr. T. wants to know why you didn't hit that nut with your club?"

"To tell you the truth, I tried to but couldn't. I also thought I could disarm him manually, which I did, without cracking his skull and maybe getting blood—"

"You thought, you thought. Did you also think that if he knocked you cold with that cigarette thing he then might have grabbed your club and come after us? You thought. Well Mr. T. and us think you're not right for this work, I'm sorry. I even think I convinced him we got to have a guard with a gun the way things are going here. He wants you to call your Mr. Gibner."

I phone Gibner and he says "Tom, what am I going to do with you? Because you do such good work, even great. You stop thieves like nobody I've seen and you look strong and presentable and you've proven yourself no thief. But you don't use your club. That made us look very unprofessional again, very. Look, finish out the day. It's okay with your boss, and then Monday a little before midnight be at this building address I'll give you to work as a guard there. You won't have to use a club but will have to carry one. You'll be mostly show, because just a guard in the lobby is enough to keep potential troublemakers away."

"I thought you said I'd only work days."

"For a few weeks work evenings. Then, in that time, you think you can swing a club again but at someone's arm or head when it's warranted, I'll put you back in a store. You think you can't, then it's apartment buildings and nursing homes from now on. Pay's a bit less there, despite the occasional midnight-to-eight shift, but that's because there's none of what we call 'possible battle pay.'"

I say "All right, but only because I need the money," and Monday night I'm at the apartment building a half-hour before my shift's to begin to learn what I'm supposed to do.

The head of the tenants' association shows me around and says the tenants are paying my entire salary. "The landlord's a cheap S.O.B. He doesn't live here, that's why he can act like that. We were getting a burglary a month and mugging every other before we started patrolling the place days and hiring a guard for after midnight. What they did to break in was ring a number of names on the intercom till someone without asking who's there let them in. When the tenants stopped letting in people this way, the intruders broke the door panes or locks to get in or just waited in the vestibule for someone to rob or followed them in from the street. What happens now is anyone in the vestibule who doesn't have a lobby door key has to get past the guard. You ring the tenant the visitor wants and the tenant has to personally give you the okay. The tenant doesn't or isn't in, the visitor has to leave. If a tenant doesn't have a key, ask for his ID. We issued everybody one with his picture on it. If a tenant says he forgot his ID and nobody in his apartment is home, or you have trouble with someone that you can't handle alone, call me in 7 B no matter what time at night and I'll be down in a minute. If I'm not in, here's another tenant's name to ring. One or the other of us will always be home, and if we're not, you'll be given the name of a third."

Except for the bad hours and little periods of boredom, it's a very easy job. I sit in a comfortable lobby chair facing the vestibule door and read or listen to a radio that man in 7 B loaned me. When I have to go to the bathroom I put a sign he gave me on the lobby door that says "Be back in 30 seconds. Premises also patrolled by attack dogs," which isn't true. For lunch the tenants' association left me a thermos each of coffee and milk and two very thick meat sandwiches on good bread and an apple.

The people who enter the vestibule are mostly tenants with lobby door keys who stop to introduce themselves and ask my name and say how glad they are to see I'm not asleep like the last two guards usually were. One tenant says if I don't like my sandwiches or prefer tea to coffee the association's food committee will change them. For the few visitors who come I open the lobby door, ask who they want, ring the tenant on the intercom in the vestibule and the tenant gives the okay. The one time the tenant wasn't in, the visitor said "Thank you" to me and went away.

A week later around 2 A.M. a man comes into the vestibule and is about to ring one of the intercom bells when I yell "Hold it" and get up, club sticking out of my side jacket pocket, open the door and ask who he wants.

"It's okay, I can ring it myself."

"I'm sorry, this is strict building policy. Tell me who you want and I'll ring the apartment for you."

"Fabor. Tell her Arkin's here."

I ring Fabor in 14K. A woman answers and I say "There's a Mr. Arkin downstairs, ma'am."

"I don't want to see him," she says. "Don't let him up. He's crazy. He's worse. He knows he's not supposed to come here. And please don't call me again that he wants to come up, which he will, because I won't answer again tonight. Thanks, Thomas."

"The lady says she doesn't want to let you in," I say.

"She wants to, don't tell me. Now let me past."

"Excuse me, but she says no. She told me specifically."

"Call her back and let me speak to her."

"She also said not to call back and that if I do she won't answer. You want to talk to her, do it from an outside phone."

"The nearest pay phone's three blocks from here. I'm speaking from yours."

He reaches for the intercom. I say "Please, don't make trouble. She said no and means no, so I think you better go."

He rings her bell.

"Now I said not to."

Rings it several times. "Marilyn," he says into the speaker. "It's me, Arkin, let me up."

"Please, you're making me look stupid with her. She'll complain to the association that runs things here that I'm not doing my job. I can get fired because of her. Every tenant's my boss."

"That's your problem." He rings her bell and I push his hand away from the intercom.

"Don't touch me," he says. "That's a warning."

"Then don't ring her bell again. That's my job."

"The hell with your job." He rings her bell, keeps ringing it as he says into the speaker "Marilyn? Marilyn, dammit, will you ring me in? You're there. You can hear me. I have to speak to you, okay? Marilyn!"

I take his arm and try to walk him away from the intercom to the street. He throws my hand off and swings at me twice. I sidestep the first but can't the second and he clips me on the chin. I fall against the wall, legs wobbly, think I'm about to drop when I see him coming at me with a real vicious face and his fists raised. I get straight on my feet again, feel for my club, see it on the floor, kick it across the room, run to it and pick it up and hold it above my head and say "Don't make me use it, will you?" He charges over and swings at me just as I swing the club at his arm, but his fist gets in the way and I hit it instead. He shouts in pain, grabs his fist, clenches his teeth, says "Christ . . . damn!" edges back to the wall he had me flat against before and puts his hit fist over one eye and open hand over the other and starts crying. Then big heavy awful coughy sobs from the throat and tears now also coming out from behind his fist and hand and dropping to the floor.

I ring 7B and tell Mr. Samuels to come right down. "I think I have . . . just hurry." Arkin now has his back to me, holding his fist, crying a normal cry again and mumbling things I can't understand.

Mr. Samuels gets out of the elevator. "What happened to your face?" Then he sees Arkin and says "Oh, that guy. Mrs. whatever-her-name on the fourteenth used to come in with him when I was on lobby duty, but I haven't seen him for months. He attack you?"

"I'll tell you later." I put my hand on Arkin's shoulder. "Hey look, I'm really sorry. I did everything I could not to, but you forced me. I hope it's not broke, though anything I can do now?" He just cries. "Then I think you better go. Right?" I say to Mr. Samuels. He nods. I take Arkin's arm. "Maybe you want me to phone a taxi for you."

"We have no phone here," Mr. Samuels says.

"Your apartment."

"Just let him go. It looks bad and one of us goes upstairs to call, the other will be left with him alone.

"Then no phone, Arkin. You better just go yourself or maybe you want me to walk you to the street for a cab."

"I'll be okay," Arkin says. "Excuse me. I was really stupid. And this hand. I can't believe it," and he wipes his face and leaves.

"I really do feel lousy about clubbing him," I tell Mr. Samuels. "But it seemed like he wanted to kill me at the time."

"If you thought he did, then I guess nothing else you could have done, though lucky it wasn't his head. Since it's the tenants who employ you, I'm sure we could also be sued. Wait here a minute."

He goes upstairs, returns with some ice for my chin and a can of beer for me, then goes back upstairs. I stay the rest of my shift. One of the tenants relieves me at eight o'clock and I go home, try and sleep, can't, and call Mr. Gibner.

"Listen, I don't know about this security work anymore. When I club someone I feel bad about it, and when I can't club them when everyone thinks I should, you feel bad about it. I just don't know what to do."

"Could be this guard work isn't your line, that's about all I can say."

"Maybe it isn't. If you don't mind I don't think I can even finish out the week in that building."

"All right, if that's the way you want it. Though believe me, chances of your having to raise that club again there for the next few months are just about nil, but anything you say."

72

I bring my uniform and club to him, get my pay, and start looking for work in a totally different field. By three, after a few interviews and no luck, I'm exhausted and I go home and sleep till around the same time the next day.

LOVE HAS ITS OWN ACTION

I met Beverly at a Mediterranean resort town between Barcelona and Tarragona—bumped into her actually as we had both been reaching for a pink pindar shell one rarely finds in this area and which we had been searching for doggedly, when our heads collided. We laughed about the accident, felt the bumps that had been mutually produced on our foreheads, were glad we both spoke English so we could apologize and joke intelligibly about the collision rather than stumble along in broken Spanish to the frustration of ourselves and the stranger we were addressing. I gave her the pindar shell, though it was rightfully mine in that I saw it first and in fact had my hand on the shell when our heads came together, and invited her for coffee at a cafeteria that overlooked the shore. In a half-hour it seemed as though we'd known each other for months. Our interests were much the same, and both of us remarked, almost at the same time, that such open personal happy conversation had never come as quickly or easily with anyone else.

That evening we slept together and while I lay in bed drinking a glass of wine, Beverly noiselessly beside me with her arms wrapped around my legs, I thought that this was the woman I was going to remain with for probably the rest of my life. She had everything I had ever found desirable in a woman: intelligence, understanding, a good nature and sense of humor and was thoroughly feminine, seemingly talented and self-sufficient and she very much appealed to my groin. After a week of sharing the same hotel room and during the days hiking to small villages and Roman ruins in the area and picnicking and making love in out-of-the-way caves and grottoes along the sea, I proposed to Beverly and she said "Of course" and nonchalantly returned to finish sewing back a belt loop on my blue jeans, as if what I had asked her had for days been comfortably settled in her mind.

We spent a week in Granada, staying at its most luxurious castle turned hotel and fantasizing ourselves living alone in the Alhambra and taking great exotic baths together in its enormous basement tubs, and then flew back to the States and announced our marriage plans to our respective families. Everyone was exhilarated with the news. My brother said I had landed the catchiest of catches, my best friend told me that Beverly was an appallingly beautiful and brilliant young woman and that regardless of our twenty-year friendship, if she and I ever separated he would be the first person to offer her his loving hand.

The wedding was planned for the following month, and after all the invitation cards had been mailed and some checks and presents had already been sent to us, Beverly told me she was getting cold feet. She said she had had a few dreams of how she had practically killed herself after learning I had been unfaithful to her with her closest friend. I told her to push the thought right out of her head: I had loved and been intimate with several women in my life but each one I had been faithful to, even—during a two-year army hitch—to avoiding the brothels of Bangkok and Tokyo and California, since at the time I was engaged to a woman in New York. She said she was very glad I felt this way and so of course the wedding would go on. But two days later I received a telegram from her saying the wedding was definitely and irrevocably off: she still got dreams and premonitions I was going to be unfaithful to her, and because of her strong religious background and close family ties she would never be able to go through such a deception without seriously hurting herself, and in particular not one involving her husband with her dearest friend.

I became extremely depressed. In two weeks I would have to return to teaching Language Arts in a city junior high school and I wasn't in the mental and emotional shape for the job. I rented a car and drove to the Smoky Mountains and camped out for a few nights, fished, hiked, read, swam, had a quiet thoughtful time. Beverly was gradually being released from my mind. One thing I resolved was that the next woman I fell in love with, as I had learned with Beverly that there wasn't any greater feeling than being in love and having it totally reciprocated, would have all the good qualities Beverly had and one she thoroughly lacked, and that was an utter confidence in her man.

One afternoon while I was fishing on the lake I heard a woman screaming for help from about forty feet away. I paddled over to her, handed her my oar and told her to hold on to it till I was able to lift her safely into the canoe. She had gotten a leg cramp while swimming she said as she rested in the boat—thought she was going to drown for sure, and then she fell asleep from exhaustion. I shook her, as I wanted to know which side of the lake she wanted to be paddled to, then gave up and brought the canoe back to my dock. I carried her to the grass and placed a blanket over her. She woke, smiled, and said I had very pretty teeth and eyes and that she greatly admired my mustache, and asked if I could hold her awhile as she was very cold. I held her, she felt cold though firm and nice, she kissed my cheek, joked about how this Latter-day Saint had finally found her latter-day savior, said that she does meet people in the strangest of places, oh yessirree, and held me tight till she fell asleep in my arms.

When she awoke she said she didn't want to return to her boyfriend and friends across the lake. "I decided I want to be with you: cooking, cleaning, rolling up your sleeping bag and scaling and boning the fish you catch, I'll try not to be in the way—I promise," and I said I was feeling very strongly about her too. I liked her directness, small cute body and adorable young face and ridiculous unconventional chatter and ways, and after we cooked dinner I told Shannah about Beverly and the exact reason I was camping alone. Shannah said that Beverly had obviously been too rigid and uncompromising a woman for me and so I was far better off without her. She said she would live with me and have my children without marriage if I wanted—that I could have as many women as I liked during our relationship and she would never complain. I told her I wasn't quite ready to get involved again, though we could write one another and if we both still felt the same way in two months then we could meet in Washington or Richmond and really get acquainted. Shannah agreed, said she now saw there wasn't any good reason for rushing into a new love affair herself, and I called a taxi from the camp grocery store and we shook hands and said goodbye. I went for a swim, and when I returned to the site I found Shannah sleeping on top of my sleeping bag, a note pinned to the blanket over her saying she had already been separated from me too long and besides her boyfriend was a bore. I snuggled next to her, she laughed, roughed up my hair, said let's both get into the bag and make like a couple of crazy Humminggay heroes, and we got inside the bag and after a bit of uncomfortable squirming found a relaxed enough position for making love.

Shannah moved into my apartment with just a valiseful of her poetry and clothes. I started teaching that Monday, happier than I had been since the night I proposed to Beverly. A couple of days into the term I saw a very beautiful young woman in the teacher's lunchroom whom I almost instantly desired as much as any woman I had known. There was something about her look—this bored placid look compared to the easy-to-please expression of Shannah's and the often frightened bewildered face of Beverly's, and I was also attracted by her hair, which was long, silky and blond compared to Shannah's thick bright red locks which hung to her shoulders and Beverly's shiny black pageboy. Her body was shapelier than Shannah's and longer than Beverly's, though all three women were equally attractive in different ways by any standard other than

77

perhaps some strait-laced ones, and had strong legs, delicate-to-sensual features, tiny waists, graceful necks, high chunky buttocks and slender hands.

This woman looked at me, emitted an expression that wholly disapproved of my staring, and went back to sipping her ice-cream soda, which stimulated me even more. I sat at her table and asked what grade she taught. Seventh, she said, and I told her I taught the same group of monsters and that most days last year they had sent me home sick and tight in the head and belly and very often close to tears. She said she thought that might happen to her also, though truthfully she had only just begun to teach, and loudly drained the soda from the bottom of the glass till a strawberry from the ice cream got caught in the straw. She said her name was Libby and I said "Well, Libby, I don't know how you're going to respond to what I'm about to tell you though I suspect all your composure and reasonably good feelings to me will dissolve the moment I say what I feel most compelled to say, but I'm absolutely stuck on you—hooked is more the word I mean, and have been from the second I saw you sitting here sucking up this soda, and that I've never had such an immediate feeling for a woman and I ain't just putting you on." She said that what I was saying was both juvenile and absurd, and excused herself and left the room.

I returned to class and was feeling dejected when a student entered the room with a note from Mrs. Redbee. Who, I asked, and he said "The pretty teacher from upstairs with the long blond hair and you know," and he gestured with his hands and chest to describe Libby's fairly large breasts. I tore open the envelope, and the note from Libby said she was very sorry she had been so abrupt before, she had never known how to react to honesty directed straight at her, if that's what it was, but for one thing she was married, for another she had two children of her own, for a third she thought she felt the same way about me, had, in a sense, from the moment she saw me sitting there nibbling away on my runny egg-salad sandwich, and that really turned her life into an unwanted dilemma, because when she left for work today she was feeling intensely in love with her husband, so what should we do? And what about me—the same truth now: was I married, engaged, did I have any kids?

I sent back a note with one of my students saying I wasn't engaged or married but living with a woman who up till the time I last remembered leaving her warm and wet in our morning bed—and I had recalled that delicious image during every class period break till lunch—I loved more than any one person on earth. She sent back a note saying we both apparently faced the same problem with probably the same brutal consequences if we followed our impulses and so it seemed best we should forget whatever romantic feelings we might have for one another as life was too troublesome an affair to contend with as it was. My return note said I thought she was right, indubitably inexorably immemorially right, and that accompanying this note was a photostat copy of my lesson plans for the year, as I figured she might use them since she was an inexperienced new teacher teaching the same grade and subject I taught. She sent back a two-by-three-foot manila envelope, and inside was a note the size of a fortune cookie message that said "Stick all classified material in this envelope and burn." I laughed so hard I cracked the class up. After I restored order and provided the class with more dictionary words to look up and define at their desks than they could do in five periods, I sent two students to Libby's room with a large carton filled with three more cartons of progressively smaller size, and inside the smallest carton a note that said "Missiles deactivated; explosives under control."

We met after dismissal at the teachers' time clock. Libby said she was glad the fire was out though after giving it some thought she really didn't think we were all that combustible, and then looked for our timecards in the card rack and punched out for both of us. We parted at the bus stop, agreeing that as long as we were teaching in what the city considered a problem school, we should remain, for the mutual protection of ourselves and discipline of our classrooms, helpful colleagues to one another.

That evening I spoke to Shannah about Libby. I only mentioned over dinner that I had met this fairly attractive female teacher today who had just started in the profession and had a lot to learn, but

Shannah quickly flew into me as to what I really wanted to say. "Nothing more to it than that," I said, "except for the fact that maybe we were unusually pleasant and considerate to one another for teachers," but Shannah said "Come on, Cy, out with it, where's the old honesty, I already told you I wouldn't mind your sleeping with three brand new teachers as long as I'm the only one who has your love." I told her there had been nothing more between Libby and me except for a momentary infatuation, but Shannah screamed back "You're in love with her, you bastard, I can see it all over your ugly dishonest face," and when I said that perhaps I was in love with Libby, she said "Then don't think I'm going to stay here while you're sulking and pining away for some bitch you'd rather be with, no boy, not me," and she went to the bedroom to pack her poetry and clothes. She returned to the table while I was finishing my dinner and said "I'll stay, you know, if you guarantee me your total committed love," and when I said I couldn't give that when it was requested of me, she borrowed a hundred dollars for a hotel room and left the apartment. Then Libby called, said she had accidentally blabbed out to her husband about this fairly attractive male teacher she met, and, after he had pumped it out of her, about that fleeting five-minute nice-feeling time she had had with me. Her husband became so enraged, as she had unwittingly said all this in front of her children, that he demanded she move her flighty carcass out of the house that instant, and did I know of any place she could stay?

Our living together caused a minor scandal among the faculty and school administration. Eventually the principal told us that because of the large student interest in our affairs and the parental concern about the effect such alleged teachers' moral laxity might have on the children, one of us would have to leave. Libby settled on my working, since I had gotten her pregnant a few weeks back and she was more than satisfied to stay home reading and enjoying her pregnancy and whatever she could do around the house for me.

That was a very beautiful time in our lives. We never had a fight, never a serious misunderstanding. Every time we got even slightly ticked off at one another, the less emotionally upset of us would say "Let's talk the damn thing out," and we would get whatever was bothering us out into the open before it overwhelmed us inside and made us explode. Then the baby dropped, the labor pains came and went and stayed, and I drove Libby to the hospital and waited in the waiting room while the baby was being delivered. A few hours later a nurse told me my wife had just given birth to a healthy cheerful seven-pound-six-ounce boy baby. I said that was nice, very nice indeed, and my legs tottered and I told her I was about to faint. The arms that guided me to the couch were gentle and strong, the hands that stroked my forehead and nose more knowing and softer than any that had ever touched me. In my semiconsciousness I imagined these same hands skimming over my entire body, giving me more physical pleasure than for the first time I could possibly stand. It was the nurse. She was towering over me, more than six feet of her, and she was saying "It's all right, Mr. Block, your wife and son are as well as can be." I held her hands, said they were soft, very comforting, she was a good nurse and she said "Thanks kindly, as I don't often get roses thrown at me like that." I told her that Libby and I weren't married because her divorce hadn't come through yet, and she said that wasn't very unusual these days with what she had read and heard about and in fact she had the exact opposite problem as me in that she was very much legally married but her husband didn't want any children. I said I loved kids and unlike Libby I wanted to have a half dozen more of them and that I thought it was a pity about her husband because I felt she'd make a superlative mother with those comforting hands and empathic disposition and because she was in such a selfless if not self-demeaning profession and also because of her body—I meant because she looked so strong and healthy to me that it seemed she could give birth to many babies and even three or four at a time. She said that come to think of it she was quite strong and healthy and that also being my nurse in a sense she was giving her most thoughtfully considered medical advice that I have a coffee with her downstairs, since we both looked like we could use one.

After coffee Regina said she lived nearby and her husband was at the first of his two consecutive jobs he held to stay away from her and that my wife wouldn't be ready to see me for a few hours yet so

"Hot Chocolate"

why didn't I come to her place for a nourishing breakfast and some small talk. I went gladly as I was very much taken by Regina. She was so powerful yet tender, gaminelike pretty in a big physical way. It was exciting merely to stand beside her and think what I could do with a woman with such an immense perfectly proportioned body and legs that had the length and strength of a champion high jumper.

Regina served me sausages and eggs, sat beside me on the couch stroking my hands as I stroked her hair and asking if I had any post-faint effects. Then she said she knew she could lose her hospital job for saying this to a man whose woman she had just assisted in the delivery room, but she was a compulsively truthful type so here goes: possibly nothing but she was drawn to me not only intellectually and wanted to make love right now and she was sorry but that was how she felt and if I had any objections to what she just said she would understand perfectly if I left the flat without saying a word, though if I wanted to be carrried to bed as she had to do with her near-impotent husband most times then she would try and understand that minor quirk too.

She was the most imaginative, inexhaustible and relaxed woman I'd ever known in bed and I didn't want to lose her—that was my first thought after she fell asleep. I felt so secure, healthy and strong with her that I thought my feelings for her went beyond my previously held conceptions about love: she was a total physical experience who could help me attain mystical heights during and right after our lovemaking peaks, though Regina had simply refered to us as two very normal good love-buddies. In the time between our shower and second breakfast we decided we could never leave each other nor have the heart or words to tell Libby, Regina's husband and the school and hospital administrations about our impossible-to-describe physical-love relationship, so the one alternative was to pack up some clothes, send Libby almost all the money we had with a promise of more to come, and go to another area to live out our lives as lovers and have half-a-dozen children. I wrote Libby a letter saying I hoped she would understand,

Regina left a note for her husband saying her leaving was partly a result of his back-to-back jobs and stomach-to-stomach indifference, and we cabbed to the train station and boarded a train that would take us to Canada and our new citizenships.

About two hours out of the city Regina asked if I wanted to go with her to the dining car. I told her that just for now I wanted to be alone with my thoughts about Libby and the child, and she said she knew what I meant: she was luckier than I in that she was leaving nobody behind. Regina left, I closed my eyes and tried to call up the image of an unpregnant Libby and our newborn child, when a woman asked if the seat was taken. I said the one beside me was but the two across from me weren't, and the woman sat down, she was of a strange racial mixture that was unidentifiable and fascinating and beautiful, crossed her legs, these extremely graceful and shapely dancer's legs that I suddenly imagined wrapped around my neck and belly, and looked out the window. I couldn't stop staring at her and finally said "I'm sorry, I'm staring, I don't normally stare at women, no that's not true, I stare a lot, and don't even listen to me if you feel I'm annoying you, I'll change seats in fact if you'd prefer that, but listen, I think you're spectacular, your face fascinates me, your body staggers me, I've always wanted to paint and with you I'd do nothing but spend the next ten years painting every part of your face and body, no all of this is such blatantly corny rot and what I'm going to say next might even sound more ludicrous to you, but listen, something's come over me, overrun and overwhelmed me, how does one go about saying this to a woman: the moment you sat down I knew that I had never felt so excited about someone in my life."

She said "Well now, that's all very interesting and such and especially when this elaborate confession comes from what appears to be a moderately sane, intelligent and handsome man, but I must rely on the phrase that you know nothing about me," and I said "Feelings, instincts, impulses, they're always more reliable than knowing and knowledge and they tell me to say that I've never said or done anything comparable to what I'm going to say and hopefully do right now but would you, if I pulled the train's stop cord, jump off and run away with me even if I said I had had similar feelings, instincts and impulses for a woman last night only a few minutes after another woman I love very much had given birth to my first child and that the birth-giving woman is still in the hospital and the woman from last night is now in this train's dining car and about to return and sit close to me, comfy with the thought that she and I will be spending the rest of our lives together in Canada?"

"Pull the cord and find out," she said. I looked down the aisle and saw Regina pushing open the door leading to our car, her other hand holding a tray of food for me. I pulled the cord, the train jolted to a stop, Regina fell down and looked quizzically at me, the woman said "I'd say you proved something or another all right," and we ran to the other end of the car and jumped off the train.

We walked across the tracks to a diner and went inside. June said "I feel lovely, I've never felt so lovely, I've never met a man with such entrancing derring-do and guts, I have to go to the can, I'll think of you every long second I'm in there, doll." We kissed, practically knotted our tongues, she rubbed my backside and said "You feel and smell so warm and true, I think I finally got myself a winner," and danced a whirlabout to the ladies' room.

I sat at the counter. The waitress came out of the kitchen and with just her first nearly imcomprehensible question as to what I wanted to order, I felt that she was the most natural looking and acting woman I'd ever come across. Her hair was in no particular state of disorder, her skin as clean and creamy as a just-bathed little child's behind, she wore no makeup, didn't need any, no underclothes either, and her body looked as if it had completed the last stage of its development just an hour before I entered the place. She seemed completely free, unsophisticated and just naturally wise, something I wanted to become as I was now sick of my promiscuous adventures and degenerate city wit and charm, and when she said "Excuse me there," and smiled the brightest happiest most unselfconscious smile a person could give out, "but I asked what you want to order," I said "You, that's all, nothing else, just you as you are." She said "Good Jay, I haven't had one like you in here since about an hour ago when the last batch of foul-smelling horny truckers stopped by."

"But I'm serious. My woman's in the john there, but if you give me my order the way I want it then we'll be out of this joint in a flash, your apron and sneakers tossed behind you forever, and you'll never regret it, you'll always remain free and warm and happy as you are and never get overcomplicated and neurotic because I'd never allow it, we can make this life the most enriching experience possible for each other and all you have to do is give the word." She said "What's the word?" and I said "You just said it" and gave her my hand, she climbed over the counter, the cook in back yelled "Where you going, Cora, and what in hell makes you think you can be leaping over the counter like that? Now go back proper around the right way and pick up this egg order. And dammit, you know the Board of Health has serious ideas about our girls wearing hairnets—I said why aren't you wearing your hairnet, Cora?" but we were past the screen door, June was still in the john, we ran across the road and stuck our thumbs out and the first car coming our way stopped for us and the driver said "Where to?" I was immediately taken with his forceful intense looks, his dark hair down to his shoulders and his lean body, and once in the car with the door just shut I said "Would you go into collusion with me and drive me to the end of the earth if need be and even continue to respect and love me though I'm about to ask you to tell this diner beauty here who I love as I've never loved anyone in my life to get out?" The man said "I was really only going to the store for a six-pack and bag of corn chips but I probably would, yes I would."

He stopped the car, Cora got out and said how throwing away her apron and new white sneakers had been about the most goddarn stupid suggestion on my part because now it would cost her a whole mess of money to replace them if she ever could get her job back, and slammed the door and crossed the road and stuck her thumb out for a ride back to the diner. I felt bad about Cora, but being with the person I loved I knew that everything would turn out all right, that love had its own actions, that when one loved there was always understanding, that love was surely the only way. We drove westward and the coutryside and mountains and bright blue sky beyond and really life itself had never looked so glorious.

CUT

They want to take my leg away. Cut it off just a little below the hip. Gangrene's set in around the ankle. Spread to the heel and now shoots of it to the skin. Not much blood circulates down there because the aorta's clogged at the knee and calf. Black tissue they call the cancerous stuff. My wife said to me what else can you do? I said anything better than that. She said the only alternative was the implant but it just wouldn't take. A fibrous artery to bypass the blocked spots and get some more blood flowing to the foot so the gangrene would dry up. I'm seventy-five. The real arteries weren't strong enough to stretch far enough to meet the implanted tube, the vascular surgeon said. Or something like that. And that or your life. Plain as that. Horrible as that must sound to you both. Sorry as I am to be so frank. Well I'll at least walk some more before I go. You won't walk for more than a month and probably less. The gangrene's spreading too fast. You mean the black tissue, I said. Call it what you want, he said. Endless trouble's what I'm calling it, though the worst part of the worst dream I'm now waking up from is what I'd like to call that rot. They all agree. Vascular man, internist, urologist who operated on me to have my prostate removed. That's what I originally came in here for. I was fine after that operation. Learning to urinate like I used to. Three days away from home. When my wife noticed two ulcers from the friction burns caused by the postoperative surgical stockings they'd bound around my feet but too tight so I wouldn't shoot an embolism in bed. They said complications like the embolisms they prevented and ulcers they weren't smart enough to avoid by simply removing my stockings at night often happen to men of my age. And because I'm diabetic and my arteries are crummy, the ulcers wouldn't heal. Gangrene set in and spread. But I've been over that route. Those murderous black shoots. And they only gave my wife fifty-fifty I'll survive the operation and nobody's promising my condition won't get worse and worse if I do. I stick my wrist with the vascular man's scissors, then the other. Then the blood flows. Better than getting a leg sliced off. Then my head flows. Better than dying like a what? Sitting outside in front. Trouser leg pinned to my behind by two extra-safe diaper safety pins. In time the surviving leg sliced off. Till I'm sitting in front like a what? Like a what? That's my wife standing by the bed. Comes in every day at noon and here she is at ten. Tough luck, lady, I try to say. She's ringing, screaming. Running, in the corridor screaming. A nurse comes. Tough luck, I want to say. Runs outside the room and yells call the resident. Too late, I say. And I'm so sorry for you, dear.

The strange thing is what made me come in when I did. I had a feeling. It sprung from a dream. I couldn't sleep last night and so like the doctor said, I took a pill. Fortunately I did. Because I fell asleep and dreamt of Jay taking his life with pills. I woke up frightened and called the floor he's on and she said everything's fine, no complaints from 646. I asked if she could go in and check. She said she's both the charge nurse and the one who gives injections tonight. And that she only has one aide and he's downstairs looking for linens for tomorrow and won't be back for an hour, so though she wishes she could she can't. I told her I'm coming over to check him then. She said I can't come over till regular visiting hours at eleven and then all right, she'll check. She checked. Sleeping like a baby, she said. I felt much better. Only a dream, I thought, and I went back to bed. But I still had to get to the hospital earlier than visiting hours began and get a special pass to go up as I still had this feeling he might take his life. When I walked in his room I nearly passed out. Fortunately I didn't. He's still in a coma but out of danger, which is why I can write to you as lucidly as this and with not so much emotion where I can't. You were always the best one in the family for that and nobody else now is around. I of course hope all is well at your own home and my love to Abe and the kids.

And then back to back another one. Yesterday someone jumps from the tenth. A patient. Not mine, but why'd he jump? Learned he had incurable cancer. Who told him? The question should be why was he told? But they did. Okay, we'll forget about that mistake. But out he went. Put on his bathrobe so he wouldn't catch cold. Very methodical. Two neatly arranged instructive notes. Don't do this and do that. So stupid to tell the patient, even if there's nothing left to be done for him here and no other place for him to go. Walks from the third to the tenth, so he at least had the strength for that. Though it might have taken him two hours, which could give the hospital an even blacker eye. A visitor downstairs sticking a quarter in the meter said he saw the man bounce. Up about three feet in the air and then of course just stayed there. And now this one. Though maybe I'd do it myself. Lose a leg at the hip? No real chance of recovering even from that surgery, he being diabetic, arteriosclerotic, seventy-five and with Parkinsonism as well. I did my best with his wrists. The nurse was very good. The man was smiling all the time. Maybe that's part of his neurological disorder. At last, he also kept repeating. At last what? I finally said, though that repetition could also be part of his Parkinson's disease. His wife got so hysterical we had to hold her down to administer sedatives. We're not supposed to, as she isn't a patient here and naturally signed no release, but she took it very well. What a day. What a day. God only forbid the irony of another patient trying to kill himself. I don't mean irony. I don't even mean coincidence. I'm talking about some link of chance events which God only forbid happening in threes.

He was such a quiet man. Well, still is. Never used the bell once. Even when he had to. So he messed himself. I used to get angry at him. Ask why he didn't buzz for the pan. He said he knows we're busy. Thought he could contain it till we came in on our own accord. Extra considerate like that. It's terrible. Working here you grow hard to these people sometimes. Like they're just very little people for all the money they have. Who have to be washed and watched but not remembered. Or else you think they're just animals of the worst sort. Who mess their own nest. I've seen them do that and playing with it in zoos. Gorillas. Animals who stand up like that with intelligence. But he was different. Such a decent man he was. There I go speaking again like he's dead. Maybe he is. Maybe the dark spirit of death is trying to give me news. His or the hospital news in general. They brought him to intensive care. Who I've heard have about given up hope. Right here. Jab jab. Nice and deep too. Not just a threat. Give me this or I'll do that. Oh no. I hate scenes like that with his wife. I was there soon after she first saw. I can do anything. Cleaning up the filthiest dentures or out the oldest bags. Dealing with the most unsightly sores and smells. You name it. Everything. Throwing up their bowels. Peanuts to us. Human garbage men. But the scene of someone crying for the near or dead I can't take. I choke up too. The end's the worst. We're not all rough and hard. Smoking cigarettes in their rooms. Relatives shouldn't be allowed in hospitals anymore. No, that's silly to say. Actually they can be a great help. Pitching in for some of what we can't. But if I had a list of patients I liked best? His would be up at the top ten. Fourth. Maybe third. The top three left me some blessings in their wills. But he was so cheery till he heard. And it was partially our fault. We should have been more careful with those socks. Even the cleats got stuck in his skin. But if the doctors weren't? Then who would expect us? But he never put us to blame. Forget the wills. First. Right up there second or first. He said that's fate. Not by design but by accidents. Said this right to my face. And not just to please me you know. I'm going to call I.C. to see how he's getting along. I was going to say if they tell me he's dead I'll die.

So the old man's gone and done it. I'd say it was almost a courageous act. And I don't want any looks at me like that. You even know what it takes to slash your wrists? Not that I'm not glad you don't know, though I once tried doing myself in. Worse than slashing myself also I thought, though don't look so scared. I wouldn't try it again. Though why should I be so confident to say never I don't know, though I surely have no plans for it now. Threw myself in front of a subway train. It was moving at the time too. Better than moving it was going at almost top speed, which is why I chose it, though I don't know why. Meaning I don't know why I actually tried it. I was eighteen. Very morose young man, a depressive-depressive. Felt nothing was going right or even would go anything but wrong, though how could I have been so right at such a young age? I also had incipient belated acne and the first half-inch of premature hair loss, but that's how strongly I then felt. I fell between the rails. Does all this seem like a lie? Tried catching the train as it shot out of the tunnel at the start of the station platform, but I must have jumped too fast. I'll never know for sure, though I certainly wasn't pushed from behind. All I got for my try was a lot of explaining to do about torn clothing and this cheek scar here from the broken glass in the well between the rails. And the perdurable image of what it's like underneath a train going sixty or so per. Uproarrrr. Powerfulnesssss. But he should have waited till late evening if he wanted to meet with success. You think he did it at ten because he knew my mom was coming in? She says no and for now he can't say but he could have heard her in the hall. She's small and her heels are always high and she has a characteristic quick clicking walk. You think I'm talking like this to pluck myself up for the unavoidable when I see my two? Mom and dad, misidentify thy son. But the question should be do I think I'm talking like this to steel myself for what almost must be faced? But I better go now as the plane leaves in an hour. I'll miss you a load, toots. The key's where it usually is. The bed's been rigged to cave in at any weight over 110. Also don't overfeed the sea horses with baby shrimp, and the mynas, turtles, lizards and dogs. The bees can take care of themselves.

No, it's not even an endemic. It's two isolated cases coming within twenty hours of each other at the same hospital but in different buildings, that's all. One because he's terminal and inoperable and the other because he believes he can't go on without a leg that must come off. What's unparalleled for us is that they happened on consecutive days. What's not uncommon is that they happen in hospitals. Running this conglomerate is satisfactorily unmanageable without dreary rumors being spread and patients and staff becoming perturbed. My advice is to drop the matter, for there's no story here other than the most witless yawny feature piece of a hospital administrator earnestly trying to squelch the commencement of a full-scale scandal and the perhaps more heart-tickling subsequent blurb of a reporter being denounced or bounced because he persisted in writing the original story.

Morris leaned over the counter and says so and so your patient? I says he was on my floor. He says was you could almost have said but still is is what you should be saying. I say I know and it was only a minor verbal oversight on my part. He says rather than only a minor oversight it was a major blunder that could have been a total medical center setback and financial clobbering. I say I think I know what you're saying and I'm sorry. He says I should hope you would know what I'm saying and I'd be a lot more than sorry. I say what else would you like me to be? He says all I ask is that you see nothing like it happens again. I say you're not saying you don't think I didn't do everything possible to see it didn't happen in the first place? He says yes I'm sure you did everything you could possibly do to see it didn't happen but perhaps what I'm saying is you didn't do enough. I say enough it was, Mr. Morris, believe me. I've seventeen rooms and there was only me and the aide Patson, because two nurses had called in sick and the other aide that day quit and every room was wanting some kind of attention. If you don't like my performance here then you can just say so. He says I've just said so. Then is that in so many words a discharge on your part? I say. It's nothing of the sort on my part since for one thing there's a nurse shortage and for another I don't even know whether I still have that power, he says. Then what is it? I say. It's an admonition, that's all, he says. A what? I say. A warning to be more careful the next time, he says. I was very careful the first time, I say.

Then be even more careful the next time, he says. As I already said I was very careful but he needs private nurses around the clock, I say. That's up to his family, he says. Then tell his family, I say. You know that even his doctor can only recommend that to his family, and goodnight, he says. And goodnight to you, I say. Was that an admonition on your part? he says. A what do you mean by what? I say. By the way you said goodnight, he says. It's what you might call a warning, I say. When it gets to be more than a warning then you can say so to me personally and in private, he says. If there happens to be a next time then I'll do that, I say, while the patients are ringing and from both corridors I can hear them bleating and I've a dozen syringes to fill and pill orders to make up and still two patients to put to bed and I don't know how many sutures to check and the linens for the next shift haven't yet shown and Patson, Patson, Patson's saying will I please listen to him a second as he's ill and a trifle woozy and could I get a replacement for him tonight or at least give him a two-hour rest after his meal?

One day someone jumps off the roof and the next day, yesterday, or the before day, he also tries cutting his wrists. You'll never get me in any hospital. Not once if I can avoid it, even if it's only to see a best friend or use their toilet. Because why go there? He goes there, right, and for one thing and gets another thing which leads to an even more complicated thing which gets so awful he's got to kill himself, and now God knows what that will lead to. At least that's what the article said. Mr. Jay from upstairs. Nice man, right? Used to sit in front of the house all day on the nice days when his wife got the energy up to walk him down. In the wheelchair, with first those clumps of the chair on the stairs past our landing and then when she got it all arranged outside with his newspapers, glasses, tissues and books, their little steps of her leading her husband down two more flights. And always a nice good nod and hello from him, and no matter how warm it was outside, in a coat. And never any unkind words from him either, if never almost ever a word. But always a smile. Bright and big in greeting and his little hands waving his fingers, and then this. All out of the blue. You go and begin and explain it. I was so shocked. I'm always shocked when I read or see on TV about people I know. Last time was that one who was what was that kid's name who got killed, I mean jailed, for riding more than a hundred in a twenty-mile zone? Driving around happily down this street we saw him in his stolen car one minute and next thing we see is him on all the local stations on the early and late evening news shows. Oh how I hated that wise-ass kid. Always did. Even when he was a kid. Always with the smirky wise look like he wanted to poke out your pupils in your eyes. Big kid he always was also, but they cut him to size. Two years it was he got, in a place to make us feel safer and him a better member of the human race. But outside of those two I can't think there was even an article or news film of anyone else we knew than ourselves with our own names in the newspaper lottery list when we were up for the million with several thousand others, but got five hundred instead. That should happen again. Oh, what a day at work. And my head cold's shifting to my chest and those unknown limb pains are back, so maybe what I need before dinner are aspirins and two glasses of your fresh orange juice first. And what do you say this weekend if he's alive we go see him and bring a little gift? Say sourballs or those baby pastries, because no matter how I hate those places I still think his being our neighbor these amount years it'd only be right.

Next door's a man dying from too many cigarettes. On the other side of me to the left's a lady who doesn't know she's having half her insides taken out tomorrow at eight. Across the hall's a boy who's spent the past year in a coma and every other hour on the hour only cries mummy mum mum. Next to him on one or the other sides' a man who tries suicide and I overheard his wife say in the hallway still has to lose his leg. In the next room to his is a woman who no specialist knows what's the matter with other than for her losing weight at an unbelievable speed. Can't eat. Next she can't even speak. Down to seventy pounds for a hefty frame and they don't think she'll last the week. Positively no visitors allowed it says on her door. I feel so ridiculous being on this floor. With only a couple of benign polyps to be removed and a little fright, though I might catch something worse from being around all these sorrowful people and horrible news. Is it at all possible to get my room switched to a less sickly floor?

Hello, dad. I'm glad you're feeling better. Listen, don't try and speak. Even if you can. They say you can hear. Can you hear? You can let me know by smiling a lot at what I say. Not that anything I'll say is funny, but I love seeing your smile. My favorite father. You're looking real well. I would've been here sooner but the weather in our country's been so bad the planes couldn't go. When they did and the kids and I got here, your airport was on strike so we had to land three hundred miles out of the way and bus in here slowly overnight because it snowed. Then I heard what happened to you. But let's forget about going into that. My husband Lanny sends his best and says he wishes he could've also flown here, and the kids their love. They're right downstairs, and after all this traveling by trains, planes, buses, cabs and subways and now only an elevator ride away, it's frustrating for them not to be let up, and unfair. The youngest I wanted to sneak in here under my coat, as he's never seen you, but if they saw him they might not let me see you again. You're their one grandpa and what they know of you is only from what I tell them and old snapshots. I don't know—but am I speaking too much or too fast? Just relax. But nod if you want me to slow down or shut up. I was saying that I don't know if you knew that Lanny's folks died in a car crash together when he was a boy. He was in it too but thrown into some soft bushes so somehow survived. Though he did get a broken neck at the time which he still gets headaches from when he stretches too far. The neck too far. Don't try it again. All right. There it is. Off my chest. But please don't make me. I mean please don't, please make me a silent promise and to yourself you won't ever try it again. I've got to know before I go. It'll also be a stigma for the kids later on. Worse than anything it'll kill mom for sure. And you and Jay Junior never got along too well, but you should see how he feels about you now. He's even postponed going back to his children and job and the new girl he's going to marry, so if for anything get out of here quick for another wedding. And when mom's here we often get calls at home from all over from people who are concerned about you. Relatives, friends, and don't worry about the leg. Whatever happens you'll still always have your good heart and head and your life. Think of new interests you can develop you never had. Music. And if I was in your position I'd read more and draw. I'd draw the doctors and nurses and how I feel about them and what I see in the room and aides and also my leg. And also my face in the mirror, looking like how I felt about myself in such a state. And in the background I'd get the pills and food and needles and curtains and even this blue urinal here. I'd make a study of it, in fact. A whole portrait devoted to it and whatever else is on the table at the time. I'd draw it all. I'd use my ambition, which you always had plenty of for that, and believe me anybody can draw. You're smiling. Is it what I'm saying's so funny or do you agree? Anyway, good. And get out. Your body's still strong. Your internist only wishes he'd be as healthy as you at your age other than for the other things and says they'll have to both run you over and then beat you to death to finally get you to go. To go from life he meant. And don't give mom any more pain. Consent to whatever the doctors say. Then everything will be all right. You'll be all right. We're not leaving from mom's till I'm absolutely sure you're all right. I'm going out for a smoke now so you get some rest. And don't pinch, oh, just sleep, just rest.

You can't believe it, Jay. When they heard at the office they all nearly cried. First the prostectomy. That wasn't so bad. With fifty percent of us supposed to get it, no man should think he'll be exempt. But that other thing. Hospitals. When I was in. Not this one, the V.A. downtown, good God what a mess. Same thing, only different. Good hospital, I'm not saying that. Our taxes have at least gone for something and our soldiers are getting treated right, but one thing always leads to the next. Went in to get a few boils on my butt cut off and what happens after that? One week is three. Pneumonia it turns out. You're telling me pneumonia from boils? Then a bad reaction to the antibiotics to cure up the pneumonia. Then I trip over my roommate's walker—an ex-major—and he breaks his other wrist and me an arm. Get me out of here, I yell, hand-to-hand combat was never as bad as this. Of course my arm's set wrong and the boils begin to return. Double pneumonia's on the way, I begin thinking, and even spare me the thought of what's following next. You think I don't discharge myself to have my new boils taken off somewhere else? Just got dressed, packed my gear, slipped down the stairway past the guards and reception desk and went to a private doctor in his office, where in a day he did it for me one-two-three. Also reset the arm and sent me home in an ambulance with a free air cushion and all the drugs in my life I'll ever need. But how they treating you, Jay? Your wife says they're making up for all their past mistakes by giving you extra-special food and service. Whatever it is you rate, I've never seen better-looking nurses. All Orientals it appears, which I think they'd make the sweetest and most competent. Everyone at work's optimistic that things are at last working out right for you. They're also getting you up a plant. Chipping in as if you never retired a hundred years ago. Even half the new help who never heard of you, and a box of chocolates as well, though I'm not supposed to tell. I told them but he's diabetic and one scimpy bite might mean so long our dearest old pal Jaysie, but Betty the great arranger there said, so, he can give the chocolates to his guests. But you suddenly look tired, as if falling asleep on me. Just go ahead, it's probaby what your body most wants you to do. Their chair's very comfortable, so I'll sit here and read my paper and maybe take a nap myself.

Good evening. Your operation's scheduled for tomorrow morning at eight. It'll take from two to three hours, and naturally you'll be totally anesthetized the entire time. After the operation you'll go to recovery room for several hours and then be returned here. You'll be getting the best after-surgery treatment available, and at home the hospital's best physical therapists and homecare nursing staff. I also understand you have an excellent nurse in your wife. I would have preferred getting your written permission, but because there isn't a day to lose with your leg, I'm satisfied with your wife's okay. I want you to know I'd never operate if your internist didn't say you're a thousand times improved since you were admitted with your urine retention and had your prostate removed. And then your self-inflicted development, which you've healed faster than expected and have sufficiently recovered from. Let's be frank. You were here when your wife asked what would happen if the implant didn't take. I said we'd discuss that bridge if we had to come to it. Well we're there now and must cross. I told you both at the time that we were one run behind with two out in the ninth with your leg and what I wanted to do, but unfortunately couldn't, was hit a homerun with a man on. Now it's a brand new ball game, one much simpler to win and with negligible trial and risk. I can't think of anything else to tell you, other than you'll be shaved tonight, wakened at seven and fed no food or fluids till tomorrow's I.V. If there are no further questions, I'll see you in the morning when they bring you up at eight.

Come on now. Breathe deep. Breathe deep. Take a deep breath. I said deep breath. Deeper. More. More. That a boy. You're all right. He's okay. Only a little scare.

It's the anesthesia. He'll be less groggy tonight. What we'll have to check daily is how his diabetes affects the thigh's healing. The Parkinson's pills we've taken him off till he's well on the road to recovery. Closest I can pinpoint for you for a discharge date is a month or so, most likely more. One thing I never like doing is sending my patients home with dressings or packings or where they still must use drugs, drains or pills.

You think he looks bad now? You should have seen him when he was wheeled in. I was the only person in the room. Your mother was having a cigarette in the lounge. Dotty was down in the cafeteria getting coffees and teas for us all. His face was greener than your shirt. We thought for certain it was going to turn blue. The man who wheeled him in didn't know what to do. I rang for the nurse. The orderly came in and slapped his face around and called for the doctors and oxygen tank. His color's about back to normal now, but for a few minutes we thought your father was gone.

Dear? Jay darling. What a morning we had. I'm so glad you slept through it all. Last night I couldn't get a single wink's sleep. Right now I'm so exhausted I could pass out on my feet. But I won't leave. Not at least till the night nurse comes. She called in saying she'd be an hour late. Something about her car stuck in the garage. But isn't it all so grand? You'll be home by the end of the month, maybe less. More than likely less. The doctor says it was a complete success. But sleep then. Close your eyes if you can. Tomorrow they'll try and give you real food.

They're all excited, Jay. With flying colors you passed the test I tell them whenever anyone asks. I reported in sick for the day. Though if they want to know the truth and dock me, then I was right here. I see all the candy's gone. What kind of vultures you got for guests? And I don't see the plant and Mrs. Jay says none was delivered. Since Betty said they said it was sent a day ago, maybe I should call her to check.

Now that you're well on your way to health I'll be leaving. I'm sure the person I left my fishes and animals with has glutted them to death. And my boss is beginning to ask what's up with me. And the kids are screaming daddy, daddy, and my ex-wife Sondra is writing oh, some terrific father you make. Next time I fly in it'll be good seeing you sitting up again. So goodbye and best wishes and I'll be phoning mom periodically to hear how you are.

Lil Bird from number ten. I would only drop by when I knew you were feeling well. Now that I know you are, I came over. The whole building misses not seeing you in front, as on the sunnier days. You were a pretty good watchdog against people who shouldn't be coming around for things that aren't theirs. Whether you knew that or not, and my husband sends his hellos also. I don't mean watchdog in the dog sense but as a watching human protector. Seeing someone there might be just what a thief needs to make the wrong person turn around. My husband likes hospitals worse than I do but thought it was our duty. I was undecided at first but happy I did and if you want anything, or the lights turned off, you tell me to tell your wife and I will.

I was your aide on the fifth when you had your prostectomy. I always like to keep posted on my old patients if they're still around here, my little boys and girls. It's fabulous what one higher floor can do, so much extra light making the room so much more brighter. And your chart reads fine and your aides tell me you've been good as gold. I'm a bit rushed today but if there's anything you ever think I can do for you, just holler. Ask for Mrs. Lake from floor five, floor five, and goodnight.

You don't know me. I'm a patient across the hall. Only some polyps removed. Now that I'm here they're giving me the round of tests. I only wanted to pop in when nobody was around to wish all the good luck to you. And also to say you got one raw deal and have every right to sue. Not that you'll collect a cent from suing hospitals. Though you will get the satisfaction knowing they might think twice about being as careless with the leg of someone else.

This must seem so very silly to you. My writing a letter like this almost a week to the day after I wrote a similar letter about almost the exact same thing. What's different this time is that instead of using a pen I'm typing on my machine. The portable I treated myself to ten or so years ago and which has almost never been touched, which accounts for it being so stuck, though it's probably also in need of a cleaning. Somehow the dirt must have seeped into it through the portable case. I'm typing to you because I have to. I can't read and writing by pen is too slow and games like solitaire and needlework and talking to strangers here just won't help. I suppose I'm making a lot of noise. Not noise like complaints but typewriter noise. Sitting here in the visitor's lounge on Jay's floor, I'm sure it must only be my mind where I think they can hear me in the patients' rooms and hallways and at the nurses' station, though the nurses have assured me they can't. And there are closed doors to this room and the walls are padded with soundproof squares and the typewriter is supposedly a silent. I haven't checked with any of the other patients, though Jay I know can't hear me as last time I looked he was fast asleep with enough drugs to keep him that way for a while. The only visitors in here I've asked said go ahead, type all you want. As you know from your experiences with Abe in hospitals, people here are much more tolerant and kind. The typewriter is on my lap. It doesn't weigh more than six pounds. The way I've balanced it I can type without discomfort and with ease. The children, thinking the worst had come and gone with their father, had gone back to their individual homes. Jay has done it again. This is the story. He tried killing himself again. He's recovering now. I caught him as I had the last time. This time lying on the floor instead of in the bed, tubes winding every which way around his arms and legs, and a needle from one in his hand with which he just managed to give himself a pinprick. I had got this strange feeling about him as I had before. I called his floor. The nurse said she couldn't check since she was the only one on duty, but when she looked during her rounds the hour before he was doing fine. I begged her to check again. She said all right, maybe she would. Everything is still fine, she reported back to me, he's sleeping well. But like the last time I couldn't take her even rechecking him as a suitable enough answer, and certainly not since that last time, and I took a cab over. It was around 4 A.M. The woman at the hospital reception desk asked what did I want? I said I only wanted to wait in the waiting room on the first floor till the regular permitted visitor's time, which is 10 A.M. She said do as you like as long as you don't go upstairs before. I waited for about five minutes. She couldn't see anything that was happening behind her except through a small mirror. Then when she wasn't looking I climbed the five flights. A nurse followed me down Jay's floor asking what did I think I was doing going to his room? There he was. She knew now what I had come for. Saved again. He looked at me crossly. If he could have spoken I'm sure he would have insulted me and scorned. Not for long though, as they soon gave him sedatives to sleep. The nurse and I lifted him onto the bed. The tubes and needle were easy for her to replace and stick back in and the hand wound just took a band-aid. The doctors were called, but it wasn't that necessary. All they did was strap his wrists to the bedrails with bandages and assign an orderly to his room as a guard. Jay at first refused all sedatives by mouth, so they had to give it in his veins. He had done it by taking down the bedrail and rolling off the mattress onto the floor. I can understand how he feels. But the doctors told him what about your wife if you try it again or were even successful at it one of the last two times? I think he understands now. He promised to everyone he'll never try it again. But who can say? What's a promise worth these days? But once he's medically released from here I've been told to institutionalize him for life. In a nursing home or a good asylum if there's one. The government will pay the whole cost or close to it I've been told. Doctors, nurses, my friends and his few old friends and even his own children have urged me to do it. They've said mom, you can't handle that man. It'll be too much for you and ruin your own health. He has to be watched all the time. And you have the authority now, everybody tells me, as his past two attempts gave you that. But I could never be that cruel.

OUT OF WORK

An ad in the Equity newsletter says a South Dakota college has an opening for an acting coach and stage director of several workshops and Theater Arts Department plays at associate professor's pay. The position is for three years starting this September. "We are seeking a working actor, not the typical theater teacher who is teeming with worthwhile erudition but deficient in performing experience."

I send my résumé and also write: "I expect because of your Equity ad you'll get 700 to 1000 applications, many from people with a lot more stage and movie experience than I and also more experience in Theater Arts departments (mine's been limited to being a substitute teacher for the N.Y.C. Bd. of Education and taking over junior high school play productions when the regular Language Arts teacher who also dabbled in Drama was sick). But I'm applying anyway, as I need the job, feel I qualify (if you're serious about wanting a 'working' actor), and want a change of scenery. In fact, I'll probably need to have a change of scenery, since once I saw your ad I did my criminal best to stop circulation of the newsletter to every New York actor and actress I could think of who might better qualify. That ought to be some indication of my industrious nature and ability to act."

The chairperson of the Theater Arts Department writes back saying: "Initially I was put off by your efforts to stop distribution of our ad. But after receiving close to 800 applications so far, coupled with the enormous sadness of learning in one 'felt' swoop that so many gifted theater performers are out of work, I am much beholden to you to say the least, and to say the most, shamelessly overjoyed. It has taken me weeks to go through all the applications, and finally reaching yours brought a much-needed levity to the task. Perhaps because of your sense of humor and certainly because of your past active experience in the field, two accomplishments that are in short supply in our department, I would like to pursue your application further, despite your lacking the M.F.A., which we hoped for in all our candidates and which the printer left out of the ad."

A few weeks later she writes: "The three year position you applied for has been cut to two years because of a reduction in our department's funds. In this college, which is run (I might say was saved) by an ex-textile salesman who rose to the top of his field (no mean accomplishment either), the Arts take third best to Business Administration and Custodial Science, the latter having the most extensive catalogue in its category in the Midwest, and is consequently the school's main source of state and corporate aid. If you're still interested in the position, it might be helpful to know that you're now one of 32 candidates out of the original 1048 still competing for the job. Some of the more attractive candidates have since eliminated themselves for stage or screen work or positions at other colleges and universities; about a thousand applicants were rejected outright or after deep consideration for a variety of reasons; another hundred applicants applied after the stated deadline; and two of the original 34 final candidates have since died. If you become one of the five finalists, would you be willing to come here to be interviewed?"

I write back saying I'd be happy to.

A month later she writes: "I am equally happy to report to you that you are one of the five finalists. Unfortunately, because of continuing payroll cuts, the position had to be reduced to a single year, though with a possible option for a second. One correction I must make is that of the two candidates who I said had died, one wrote me saying she was 'only kidding,' though with no enucleation why. And the second said that the person who claimed to be the executor of his estate was in fact his archenemy and longstanding theatrical rival in that part of the country (and coincidentally a final candidate for the position himself) getting even on a number of old scores (some of them musical, I'm sure). I quickly eliminated all three from the competition, which might seem 'unequityable' to you, but with so many highly qualified candidates to choose from, I was snatching (you might say) at eliminative straws. Another thing, Mort: because the position is now only for a year and with no possibility of tenure even if you were asked to stay on for a second year, its title of 'Theater Arts teacher' will henceforth be known as 'actor-in-residence,' with the salary commensurately reduced to that of an assistant professor's rather than the assoc. professor's pay as advertised. And with vacant houses going for a premium in this booming college town, there'll now be no assurance of an on- or off-campus abode, which might change the title to 'actor-out-of-residence' if the person who gets the job can't find a home. (When the original 'in-residence' pun was told to me, it seemed much funnier than the above. I've always been remiss with key lines and cues, which is perhaps why I gave up acting to only teach and administrate.) If you're still interested, after all I've just said, please list two possible times you might be able to come here for a minimum stay of two nights and days between August 19th and 24th. I'm sorry to rush you like this, but the position does begin with the new fall quarter on September 3rd."

I write back giving the dates I can be in northeast South Dakota.

Several weeks after I was supposed to have been interviewed, the chairperson phones and says "Do you think you can fly out tomorrow or the next day for the interview? The job is still for one year though begins with the winter quarter now and with no possible option for a second year."

"I can come tomorrow. Do you make the flight arrangements from where you are or should I do all that here and be reimbursed when I arrive?"

"The school policy is for the interviewee to make his own traveling arrangements and be reimbursed in full if he gets the job. If he doesn't get it, the college reimburses half of all his expenses, though with both it takes a minimum of one to two months to receive."

"I'm not a gambling man, Sarah, especially with money I'll have to borrow to pay for the trip, so what are my chances of getting the job?"

"I'm sure I'm not supposed to reveal this, Mort, but the four other finalists bowed out because they didn't want to uproot their families for only one year when there was no chance the contract would be renewed. So I'd say your coming here is more to interview us and see how you like our department and countryside rather than our interviewing you."

"In that case, I'm on my way."

She tells me of the one plane I can catch in Minneapolis to get to the North Dakota airport, the closest to the college. "There's no train service to here and the one bus from Fargo leaves an hour before the plane lands, so someone will meet you at the airport and drive you down."

It takes all day to get there. Long stopover in Minneapolis, longer Fargo wait for the car. I'm put up in a student dorm, "Which would normally cost you a dollar a night," Sarah says, "but I think my department can absorb. You'll have to shell out for all the other expenses while you're here, so for reimbursement purposes keep your receipts and an exact written record of what they're for."

That night I'm to meet several Theater Arts Department people and their mates at the one restaurant in town that Sarah says serves halfway decent food. Before we go we have cocktails at her house and she gets high and her husband Ike gets a little drunk and begs off from "Old Ptomaino's to take care of my hounds who have colds and who I don't want getting lonely without me and during dinner and dopey talk just toppling over and die."

Driving to the restaurant at 30 mph over the national speed limit and about 70 mph more than her tipsiness could seem to control, Sarah says "Ike didn't come mostly because he went out for the job too. They wouldn't consider him because he had little theatrical experience except for his Ph.D. orals and the defense of his dissertation on Beckett's effect on the East Berlin years of Brecht, or was it the other way around, with Brecht on Beckett's German poems? But there's some execrable state law where it has to be a professional like you and preferably someone outside the school or we don't get those particular funds. Kind of makes me bitter, for we need the money and it'd be fun working with that shiftless slob for once, but no hard feelings, you hear?" and she turns to me for an answer and we narrowly miss a cow as we plow through the first row of a front-lawn cornfield.

The dinner talk is mostly about rifles, shotguns, the upcoming hunting season when most of the men expect to fly north and bag a couple of moose, turkey shoots, do I shoot? "No? Then trap and fish? Then what do you expect to do around here weekends if you get the job?" And movies. Quality of acting in x-rated classics, which are all they get in the area. The greasy food we're about to eat. "But great Bloody Marys," someone says, "with two shots each in them of real commie vodka, and a celery twig instead of lemon slice, so you can get some roughage too." Crime in New York. Death of the Broadway theater, rebirth of the regional. Where I'm originally from for there's an accent that's not Manhattan, which a few of them say comes from London and almost everyone detects as not from New York. "North Carolina," I lie. "So you're down home like all of us, even if you been living in that cesspool for fifteen years." *Joan of Arc, Timon of Athens,* and *Cyrano de Bergerac,* the three major Theater Arts Department productions this year that I'd be expected to help direct. "What are your ideas on Cyrano for instance? Would you portray him as a sympathetic impotent or a detestable sex-starved rogue or both? Do you think Rostand was influenced by Collodi's *Pinocchio,* which if you didn't know was written just fourteen years before *Cyrano?*" "Seventeen years," someone says. "Fourteen." "Seventeen." "Let's settle it," Sarah says, "and call it an even dozen." "Even two dozen," the person who said "seventeen" says.

Gradually a couple of the teachers or their husbands or wives get drunk and have to wait in their cars for their spouses to finish dinner and in one case both get drunk together and leave while their desserts are being set aflame. "Put ours in two doggy bags," the wife says before they go. Finally it's just Sarah drinking more but getting soberer it seems, and the scenic and costumes design professor and his girlfriend, a Theater Arts Department senior who will be starring, he says, "in one of your three major plays this year including *Cyrano* or *Timon* in drag—that is, if you don't positively mind."

"Does that mean you know something I don't, and maybe you do too," I say to Sarah, "which is that I have the job?"

"Gordon was saying if, if, if. No final decision can be made till the vice president and English Department chairman and I get together the day after you leave."

"Last winter," the professor says, "for this flambé reminds me so much of it—remember, Sarah, the fireplaces we kept glowing for seventeen days straight?—we had a blizzard so tough, Mort, that it obliterated three people in this town alone. One of them this cute-as-can-be young history and marital team from the East who'd never seen such a snow and thought they had to experience it in the raw with a walk around their little street. I don't mean they went outside in the raw, for theoretically their habiliments on any other day or night, shall I say, would have availed."

That night I can't sleep much because of the drinks or spicy food and the beer parties going on in the surrounding rooms and floors. Next day I conduct a directing class and acting seminar, both with the Theater Arts Department staff watching and commenting—"I disagree with Mort's interpretation of that walk-on." "I agree." "I don't." "You don't disagree with Mr. Silk's interpretation of the walk-on or you agree with Chuck and Faith?" "Excuse me, Professor Blen, but when I said I agree I didn't mean I agree with Chuck but with Mr. Silk"—and after lunch I'm interviewed by the English Department chairman who tells me he's been to New York City twice, both times to read papers at an MLA convention and also to see some shows. I ask what the letters MLA stand for and he says "I'll skip that remark as either being indirectly pointed or too tempting for me to respond to in the cynical rather snotty way I dislike in everyone, including myself."

"Wait, I don't want to be misconstrued, especially by you. I suppose the last letter stands for Association, or possibly Academy, but I was sincere when I said I didn't know."

"I'll accept that, sir."

I'm next interviewed by the college's vice president who holds open a thick folder with my name on it, and which has letters of recommendation and my correspondence with Sarah sticking out of it, and she says "You haven't applied for too many college jobs, have you? Though I suspect all serious people in the arts, because of what should we call it? The emotional pressures of their work and the different sort of acquaintanceships they make over the years— have to be somewhat bizarre by nature and innovative in the social ways to just get on with it, as our students say, now isn't that so?"

"I never thought there was anything that unusual about our behavior or that our pressures or the people we meet differed from any other line of work, except for a little something here or there which every profession has peculiar to its own, but you're probably right."

Later Sarah says the Theater Arts and English department faculties would love for me to give an informal reading of my favorite monologues from plays. "We have an excellent library for a college this size, and it is kind of expected of you I'm afraid."

The reading went so well, she tells me over dinner at the same restaurant of last night, "that the two departments would like to jointly sponsor a reading in the main auditorium tomorrow afternoon for the entire school and nearby communities to enjoy."

A modest admission price is charged at the door and enough money is made, she later says, "to sponsor several free poetry and play readings by lesser-known performers during the year, and even pay them a fee. We're all very grateful to you, and it certainly didn't diminish your chances in securing the job."

"Does that mean I have it?"

"Do you live alone?"

"I have my own apartment."

"Then I suggest you start thinking about getting a sublessee."

Sarah can't find anyone to drive me to the airport. Ike was supposed to but he disappeared into the woods behind their house with his hounds and quiver and bow and enough food for three days, and she, because of ecological reasons that she suddenly decided on after a bad dream last night, no longer drives a car. I phone the young woman who asked for my autograph after the reading last night and who said if there was anything she can do for me short of driving me to New York, please let her know.

"If you only called five minutes earlier," she says. "But now I'm in bed with a sick friend."

I take the bus to Fargo, which stops at about a hundred towns along the way, one for a half-hour food and rest break. In Minneapolis I miss the last plane to New York and can't make any connections till early morning, so I sleep the night in the airport lounge.

A month later I still haven't heard from Sarah. I write asking what the decision is and two weeks later she writes back "I wanted to delay answering you till another candidate confirmed his appointment to the position of actor-in-residence. After you left we interviewed one other actor and actress and felt that Hans Radish's 'performance' in the classroom was the most promising of the three, and since his acting experience is as impressive as yours, that he should get the job. Please send your receipts and a written record of what each receipt is for so I can start reimbursement proceedings to get your money to you soon as we can."

I send the receipts and written record along with a note saying "Because you misled me in stating I was to be the one interviewee for the job and that this interview was really just for me to see if I liked the job and all of you, which is the sole reason I thought I could afford to fly out there, I want to be reimbursed in full."

Following week I get a check from the college bursar for half the expenses I paid out. I write Sarah and the English Department chairman that I'm not going to cash this check till I get another check for the rest on my expenses or at least the equivalent of that money as a reading fee, and I get no response. I write the college vice president and tell her why I think I should get the rest of my expenses or a reading fee and she writes back "An impartial board has carefully considered your complaint and though sympathetic to your financial and professional situation, has decided that the college reimbursed to you all that you deserved." I then write the senior South Dakota senator and the college president and include copies of my letters to Sarah and the chairman and college vice president and her reply. The senator says "South Dakota has always been known as a fair-minded state and personally, your grievance seems just. But rather than ask for a reading fee, which might also be just if it weren't a little after the fact, I should write the president of the college asking for the rest of your expenses." I send the college president a copy of the senator's letter and he still doesn't reply. By this time it's December and I've run out of people to borrow money from and I still haven't found a job. I cash the college's check with a friend. He calls a week later and says "I have to ask you for the money back plus the bank's three-dollar service charge, as that check bounced because the college went bankrupt."

THE INTRUDER

I go into our apartment. She's being raped. They're both naked. He's on top of her but not inside. He holds a knife to her neck. I say "All right, get off." She says "Tony—don't." He says "Just stay where you are, buddy, and your girlie won't get hurt."

"I said to get off."

"Tony, don't do anything. He'll kill me. He means it."

"You want your girlfriend killed?"

"No."

"What's your name?" he says to her.

"Della."

"Della doesn't want to be killed," he says.

"Just get off and dressed and out of here and we won't make any complaints against you."

"First I get my satisfaction and then I think about going."

"Then I'll have to kill you," I say.

"Tony, don't try anything. Let him do it to me. It'll be all right."

"The lady's got a good head," he says. "I'm going in. You just stay where you are."

"Stay there, Tony."

"Get off," I yell.

"Open up," he says to her.

She opens up.

"Don't do that," I yell at him.

He sticks the point of the knife to the side of her neck. She says "Ouch, that hurts." I say "Leave her alone. What did she do to you?" He says "Then just stay there and don't leave the room or I'll cut her throat and then go after you."

"I don't care about myself."

"Be a hero, big boy, but the lady dies if you step a foot nearer."

"Please stay there," she says to me.

"I can't stay here and watch."

"Then turn around."

"Better you turn over," he says to her. "My neck's beginning to hurt from trying to keep an eye on him while I make it with you." He gets up.

"What do you want me to do?" she says.

"Get on top of me." He gets on his back. She gets on top of him.

"And now?" she says.

"Don't do anything," I say.

"Just be quiet, Tony. It'll be quick."

"It'll be great," he says to me. "And now I can have my fun and watch him both. Now put it in," he says to her.

She tries. "It hurts," she says.

"Bullshit."

"But there's pain," she says. I turn around.

"Don't you go anywhere," he says. I go into the next room.

"Tony," she says. "Come back or he'll kill me." I go back. I watch. They make love. He says "Bounce." She bounces. "Go slower," he says. She does. I put my hands over my eyes. I hear noise from both of them. Panting. Then him screaming. She screams too. I think she's hurt. I look. He's clutching her hard to his chest, squeezing all the air out of her. She's still on top of him. He holds the knife to the back of her neck. His eyes are almost closed, but he's looking at me. "Over for now," he says. He falls out. She says "Can I get up now?"

"Get up and clean yourself and then we come back," he says. "And you just stay there," he says to me, "or Della gets killed." They go into the bathroom. "Let's take a shower," he says to her. "I like them with girls. Turn on the water." She turns the water on. "Make it lukewarm." She turns the spigot and says "It's lukewarm." He sticks his hand under the water. "A little warmer." "That's lukewarm," she says. "Warmer!" She turns the hot spigot. "It's warmer now," she says. He feels the water. "Good. Now let's get in." They get in under the shower head. "Wash me," he says. "And you stand by the door," he says to me. I stand by the door. She washes him. "Now get behind me and scrub that back." She scrubs his back. "No washrag?" he says. "Do we have one, Tony?" she says. "No clean ones," I say. "Your hands will do then," he says to her. "Now wash my hair but no soap in the eyes." She washes his hair. "You got shampoo?" "Yes," she says. "Not in the eyes, though." She suds his hair with shampoo. He rinses himself off. "Wash my thing." She does. "Now yours." She washes herself down there. He gets out. "Now turn the cold water on all the way and the hot all the way off." "I don't like it cold," she says. "All the way." She turns the hot water off and the cold water on. She's shivering. He's loving it. She says "It's too cold. I can't take anymore."

"Jump out of the shower," I say.

"Does and she's dead. Now turn it all the way hot after you turn all the cold off."

"I can't." She turns the cold water off. "I'll scald myself."

"I said hot."

"No. Cold's enough." She's still shivering.

"If you make her turn it on hot I'll jump and kill you," I say.

"Remember, I still have a knife."

"And I got a table leg," and I knock the lamp off the end table next to me, take the table in the air and smash it against the wall. It breaks. A support piece is still attached to one of the legs. The other three legs are still attached to the table top. I snap off the support piece and now have my table leg. "I can split your head in very nicely with this, very nice."

"Don't, Tony," she says.

"Only if he forces you to stand under the hot in there."

"I won't mind. I mean, I'll mind but I'll at least be alive."

"You don't know if he'll let you live after that."

"I'll take my chances with him. Don't do anything. Let him do what he wants."

"No," he says. "No hot water. I was only kidding. She'll be of no use to me later on with burns. Get out of there." She steps out of the shower. "Dry me." She does. "Especially my thing." She does. "Dry yourself." She does. "Now back in the bed. And you step a few steps aside," he tells me. I do. They go back to bed.

"You," he says to me. "Get on the floor and lie on your stomach right at the side of the bed. I want to make sure I see you when I get on top of her."

I stand where I am.

"Do it, Tony," she says. I lie down parallel to the right side of the bed.

"You get on your back this time," he says to her. She does. He gets on top of her. "And you keep your arms under your head and your eyes on the floor and don't move from there," he says to me. I look at the floor. "Now make me big again," he says. I don't see anything. I hear him getting excited. "That's nice. You really do a job," he says. I hear the bedsprings. I hear them both making noises. Pants and groans. He screams. She doesn't. "Move it some more," he yells. I hear the bedsprings rattling louder. Then they stop. He says "That was good. First class. You're really good. You're really a piece I wish I had always. I wish you was my girl for a long time. I'd do it to you all the time, baby, I mean all. You'd never have complaints."

She doesn't answer. "You all right, Della?" I say.

"I'm okay. I'm getting sick of this though."

"You want me to jump him?"

"Hey, where'd you put that club?" he says. "Look up." I look up. "I'm so stupid. I forgot about your club. Where is it?"

"I left it in the bathroom."

"Tell him the truth," she says.

"Under me."

"Throw it out," he says. He has the knife on her throat.

"I can also use a lamp. One of the other table legs. My hands."

"Throw it out."

I throw it under the bed.

"Now you get up and come here and make me big and strong again," he says.

"No thanks," I say.

115

"I was kidding again. You think I'd want a man touching me there? You're crazy. But if I said your girlfriend dies if you don't, you'd do it."

"I wouldn't."

"Your girlfriend dies if you don't."

"Do it, Tony," she says.

"You see, she wants you to." I stand up. I grab him. It's like my own. I know what to do. He stays soft.

"Put it in your mouth," he says.

"Nothing doing."

He puts the point of the knife to her Adam's apple.

"Do it," she says to me. "Soon it'll be over."

I do it. I close my eyes. He gets hard. "This isn't bad," he says. "Never did it before with a guy, but not bad. Now you run it up and down with your hand while he's doing it to me." She does that. I feel her hand brush against my lips every now and then. As if she's trying to comfort me with her touch. Brushing up against my lips and under my nose and against my nose. I know her touch. I concentrate on that. "Hey, this is even great," he says. "What kings had I bet. What every man should have at least once in his life. You should have it too. Except I'd never do it to any man. Except if my girl was being threatened with a knife. My girl or baby. Only then." He comes. "Oh crap. I meant it for her. You did it too well. Both of you. My congratulations, but that's it." Her hand stops. I spit on the floor several times. "Can I go in the bathroom?" I say.

"No, just stand there."

"Let him go," she says.

"All right. Go because your girl asks for you to go. But I'm watching, so no tricky stuff in there or she gets killed."

"I know." I wash myself in the bathroom.

"Take off all your clothes and come on out now," he says. I take off all my clothes. I come out of the bathroom and he motions me to stand by the bathroom door. They're still in bed. Knife against her throat. "I suppose I should go now," he says. We say nothing. "You'd like for me to go of course." Nothing. "Well say it, goddamnit."

"Yes," she says. "We'd like you to go."

"No reason to stay here anymore," he says. "Three times. In how many minutes do you think? Not that anyone's counting. But it's enough anyway. But maybe I can get hot once more if you two do it. I'd like four times. I'd like five but I got to be realistic. But with four I can say it's really been worth it. Go on. You two do it." He gets off the bed, stands by the bed with the knife at the side of her neck. I get on the bed. "Do it with you on your back," he says to me. "That way I'll have the advantage."

"I don't feel like doing it," I say.

"Neither do I," she says.

"I said do it."

"I can't just do it like that," I say. "I'm not like you. I have to want to and I don't feel like it."

"Neither do I. Just go," she says to him. "Please?"

"I said to do it," he yells at me. "Now do it. Try. Get big. Do it to her. Then if I'm big I'll take over for you."

"But I don't feel like it."

"Rub him," he tells her.

She rubs me. Nothing happens.

"When he doesn't want to he can't," she says. "I know him."

He grabs me. Rubs me. Nothing happens. He puts it in his mouth, the knife against my penis. Nothing happens. "What do you expect?" I say. "It's impossible. Nothing, you see?"

"If I didn't have the knife it wouldn't be nothing," he says.

"Then put away the knife," I say.

"You do what I did," he tells her. He gets up, holds the knife to her neck. She does it. Nothing happens. He rubs me while she's doing it. Nothing.

"Say nice things to him," he says.

"Tony, I love you. Tony, I love it. This. What we're doing. What I'm doing. Do it. Get big. I want you to make love to me. I'm going to do it again now, so get big."

She does it. Nothing happens. "It's impossible," I say.

"It's impossible," she says. "Believe him."

"If you don't get that thing going I'm going to cut it off," he says to me.

"I'll try." I concentrate. Nothing. "Maybe it will. Wait."

"Get hard," she says. "He'll kill you if you don't. Then he'll kill me. Put your mind to it."

I concentrate. I shut my eyes. Nothing. "I'm sorry," I say to him. "I can't. But don't do anything rough. Maybe I can. Just wait."

"Don't do anything to Tony," she says. "We were nice. We did what you asked. We won't make any charges against you to the police. We won't even call them."

"Bull," he says.

"You're right," she says. "Of course we'll call them. But don't do anything now. Tie us up. Then leave."

"I want to do it once more," he says. "Four's my lucky number. Not my lucky, just a good number. And I've never done it four times in a row in so short a time. And I feel cheated. That one with him doesn't count. So I haven't even got my three yet. And three's my minimum. The absolute must. And I can't get big either. Make me big," he says to her. "Do what you can." She tries. "Everything." She tries everything she used to do to me. Nothing happens. "Both of you try on me." We both try. Things I've never done before. Knife at her neck. Nothing happens though. He stays the same way. "You're both screw-ups," he says. He stands up. "You come with me." She stands up. "You stay there," he tells me. I stand up. "I said stay."

I walk towards him. He has the knife at her back. I bend down and stretch under the bed and get the table leg. "I don't care about her life anymore," I say. "I just want to beat your brains in."

"Bull," he says.

"Tony, drop the club."

I drop it.

"You didn't mean what you said," he says. "Too bad. It would have been nice sticking it in her and then pulling it out quick and fighting you off with a couple of feints and slices or two and then sticking it in you. Maybe not nice. But different. And I could do that. I'm ready. I hope you believe that. Sure you do. And I'm very very good with this knife. So maybe you should try," he says to me. "Come on. Pick up your club and try and get me."

"Don't, Tony."

I don't. "I wasn't going to hit you with it anyway," I say to him. "Just go. Leave us alone."

"No, come on," he says. "If you don't come at me with the club I'm going to stick the knife in Della's neck."

"No." I sit on the bed.

"You want me to stick it in her neck?"

"No."

"Where then?"

"No place. All I want is for you to go."

"Just stay there like that, Tony," she says. "This will be over soon. Or in an hour. Or a day. Then it'll be over. But you're being smart. Even if he knifes me don't attack him and risk your life. Only attack him if he comes after you. But now just leave him alone. He'll eventually go."

"Don't be too sure," he says. "Come on, big boy, come try to get me with the club."

I lie on the bed, head on the pillow, arms over my chest.

"Then I'm going to put it in her back or neck."

"Please don't," she says.

"Even if you do, it'll be her neck and she'll be dead. So what's the sense of risking my life for her as she said?"

"Because you'll have a better chance to come get me and beat me over the head in the time I stick it in her neck and try and pull it out to get you. You have to think like that."

"That makes sense," I say. I stand up.

"Sit down," she says. "Lie down, Tony."

I lie down.

"You two are just no fun," he says. He gets dressed. "Don't move," he tells her. "Just stand by my side." He sits down. "Put my socks and shoes on and tie them tight." She does that. "All your money now," he says, "and his." She collects it with him following her right behind. "Now walk me to the door. And you stay in bed or try and come after me with or without the club," he yells at me.

"Stay in bed, Tony," she says.

They go to the door. I can't see them. "Now kiss me goodbye," he says.

"Oh stop the crap already and go," she says.

"You're right. You're much smarter than him. Who needs a kiss? Kiss him. He needs it." He opens the door and goes.

We don't have a phone. I go next door to call the police. Della says "I'm going to take a shower for an hour and don't want to be bothered by anyone," and goes into the bathroom. The police come. "Come out when you can," I yell into the bathroom. She comes out. Lots of questions from the police. We tell them everything. One policeman says to Della "You should go straight to a doctor." She says "No, I'm okay. I can take care of myself." We go to the police station and answer more questions and look at photos. None are of him. I say to the police we're exhausted. They say sure. We go home. That evening a circular from our police precinct is pasted on the mailbox in the vestibule and slipped under every tenant's door. It's a warning about that man today who's been raping and robbing women in their apartments in the neighborhood lately. It has a good description of him, ours along with others. Several different outfits and hats. The outfit and hat he wore today are there. The circular says he gets into the apartments mostly by telling the woman over the downstairs intercom that he's a delivery boy from a local florist with a box of flowers for her.

"Did he tell you on the intercom he was a florist delivery boy with a box of flowers for you?" I ask her.

"No, at the door."

ANN FROM THE STREET

I meet Ann on the street. At first I don't recognize her. Woman yelling "Dave?" I look. Car's coming too. We're both in the crossing and car's not going to stop. I immediately see she's pregnant and not going to move except maybe at the last moment and I pull her by the elbow closer to the sidewalk and then on it and let her go and she says "You remember me."

"You almost got yourself killed just now."

"I know, that was stupid and thanks, but you remember me. Ann from the street."

Now I know. She's much darker, has pink-tinted prescriptions on, hair cut shorter but covering most of her forehead when before it was brushed straight back, face thinner, pregnant, looks much different. "Sure. How are you?"

"Fine, and you?" Puts out her hand and we shake.

"Okay. And Ryan?"

"Couldn't be better. He's writing movies now, very big-time stuff in Hollywood. Everything seems to have worked out. But what about you, beyond being okay?"

"Things seem to have worked out there too. Three books in two years have been published and a fourth's due in June."

"Fabulous. We did get a postcard from you about something about it."

"That was about my first and second. I just finished my fifth and also a play the other day. That's why I didn't recognize you, and am surprised you did me. My eyes are a little tired. Celebrated the end of the play last night and had too much to drink."

"You just had plenty, not too much. You deserved it I guess if you finished a play. It's a long one?"

"Over full-length. That your second?" pointing to her stomach.
"First."

"Perry from the street told me so long ago that you were pregnant that it almost seems as if it could be your second."

"Perry was the first to hear, that's why."

"When—" I start to say and she says "End of November."

She looks so great, thin, belly barely a bulge though end of November's only a couple of months away, less—but she goes on. "How's you sister?"

"Great. Moved to L.A. California's changed her life she says."

"And her son?"

"Doing great too."

"How old is he now?"

"Almost thirteen."

"Thirteen?" She can't believe it. "I remember when—"

"On his scooter."

"Up and down the block. Once under someone's legs. He was always so frisky. Thirteen. Must be pretty big."

"He's getting there." I'm starting to feel depressed. Maybe from last night's drinking, which made my body today a little upset. But Ryan and Ann have been married for about ten years and have a child coming, which could make me depressed. She's so happy. And more beautiful than ever, maybe from the baby, and kind, warm, intelligent, the rest. Instead I'm by myself, no woman, no child, no past marriage, nothing like that, and no prospects, in two small rooms, and where all my relationships with women over the past fifteen years have been failures after the first few months or a year, while theirs has obviously flourished, not just stayed intact. I've seen them during the last few years eating behind restaurant patio windows in the neighborhood, laughing and gabbing and

122

holding hands. Seen them once or twice kiss each other affectionately on the street and one time a year ago or so passionately goodbye as he was getting in a cab with hand baggage and a typewriter, though at the time I was involved with a woman and doing the same things on the street and behind patio windows but not to someone I've been with for years. But she goes on.

"Then you make a living writing now?"

"Just about, but I keep my living small. Still working?"

"Right to the end. I help edit a magazine."

"Oh yeah, which one?"

"You wouldn't know it—we don't accept short stories. A trade one for beauticians and their shops. It's good work, different, only twenty hours a week, so for me perfect. Anything longer—"

"Wait, you were doing. . . "

"Hospital research."

"I thought physical-therapy work."

"Research, on hospital medical records, then writing reports on it. So the two professions aren't too dissimilar, editing and before, if that's what you meant."

"No, I was just remembering you in your white hospital suit—"

"They made us wear it for some reason. Cleanliness. Show. Something, not that I minded. It made me feel like a doctor."

"Every morning, while I was on my way to sub in junior high schools, you biking down the block on your way to work."

"Now I just walk across the park three days a week. See? Perfect."

Her face. Darkened by the sun. Looks recent. They had a long vacation someplace, maybe overseas, Greece, but some beach, probably L.A. Black hair cut prettily over her face, well done. Everything well done. Nice voice. Real poise. Beautiful smile. Five years younger than I or thereabouts. I wish I'd met someone like her ten-fifteen years ago. It'd be the same I think. I'd still love her, she me. And to have a baby in November would be perfect after ten-fifteen years of those kind of years. I don't make anywhere near what Ryan must with his films, nor could afford the brownstone duplex they bought in the area a few years ago, according to Perry, but it would've worked out. Our surroundings would've been cosier. In three rooms instead of my two. More my style. She would've stayed close. Helped and comforted me, given me warmth, body to hold almost every night when I was drifting into sleep, something I need and love. Things I'd have given her as much of if not more. Baby husband love warmth comfort body, same person all those years and happy with it. Memories shared and made the most of. All that. Would've been great. What I want but it's almost too late for that now isn't it? I want it to have happened and still to be living through it. Now it'd take years. It won't work. I've just about proven myself a loser with personal relationships. My last was disastrous. One before that almost worse. Before that only a little better. On and on back. Most women I'm now interested in say I can barely talk to them anymore. That my lovemaking's become too rushed. That I've really lost the touch. That I'm too settled in my ways. That I ought to just have affair after affair and be satisfied with that for the next twenty years or till I tire of them and then have nothing but my work. So why do I think now I could've had something like that with someone like Ann ten-fifteen years ago or even twenty? Luck at an early stage in my relationships, that's why. Plain luck.

"Well, it's been fun chatting," she says. "I'll tell Ryan I saw you."

"Do, and give him my best."

We shake hands, mine out first. I look into her eyes to catch the color of them. Can't because of the glasses except that they're dark. I've recently found I can be with a woman for months before I realize I don't know the color of her eyes except if they're startlingly blue. I drop her hand and she turns to go. "The bike," I yell.

Bike almost clips her as she crosses the street. Bike passes without slowing down. "Watch where you're going next time," I yell after it.

"She should've been watching out for me," cyclist yells back.

Ann's turned around to me, shoulders humped as if to say how dumb she was not to see the bike, waves, goes. I watch her from behind. She's got an Ace bandage around her right calf. Maybe it goes all the way up to her thigh. As a support I suppose because of the weight of the baby or leg veins or reasons I know nothing about. Continues to walk. Her hair flops. Her shoes are flat. Her dress is black, shirt blue. It isn't a dress but something like a pinafore or whatever it's called with two straps over the shoulder that button right on top of the shoulder knobs and very loose over her body, also because of the baby perhaps, black probably because of the baby too. So she won't look that pregnant, so the bulge won't show that much. It worked. She walks. Is so pretty. Voice face smile niceness kindness lovingness warmth. I picture her coming home to me. Standing there on the sidewalk my eyes still following her, I do. I'm writing. She puts a key in the lock, then the next. I hear her and run to the door. My room would have to be somewhere near the front on the first floor. I open the door same time she does, key still in the lock. She laughs. She might say "You almost pulled my arm off." "I wouldn't do that," I'd say, "I love that hand and arm too much." All of this is too much perhaps but I'd say it, I've said it, and kiss that hand and maybe go right up her arm with my lips and take the key out of the lock for her and give it to her and then kiss her neck and mouth. I'd hold and hug her. Maybe not too hard because of the bulge. It'd be our apartment alone and I might say to her then "Let's go to bed." She might even agree. Seemed like nothing pressing for her now, probably not a workday. She didn't have any packages when I met her so she wouldn't, if she doesn't pick up any on the way home, have anything to put down. I could even lift her up and carry her but that might scare her so I don't think I would. Later she might say or before we get to bed that she met someone I know on the street. I'd say "Who?" and she'd say "You. I said I'd give you your regards. No, you said to give your best and I said I'd tell you I saw you on the street."

NAMES

Finally I become depressed by her. I walk around the room. I lie in bed. I try and read. I try to sleep. I look in the refrigerator. I open the bread box. I drink. I go outside. I walk the streets. I look in the apartment windows. I look at the store windows. I go to a movie. I leave the movie halfway through. Maybe quarter way through. I go to a bar. I sit and order a drink. I stand and set my beer down and go to the washroom though I don't have to. I go because I want to walk through the crowded bar. I want someone to say hello. "Hey, how are you, what's doing?" I want someone to say. Or someone who doesn't know me but wants to speak. But no one says anything to me or looks at me as if they want me to speak. I take a pee anyway. I return to my stool at the bar. It's taken. "That's all right," I say when the person who's sitting there stands and says "I'm sorry, this yours?" The person insists. I say "Really, I don't mind standing. I like to stand." "Great then, for I want to sit," the person says. The person gets her wine. She lifts the glass. I watch her drink. Watch her set down the glass and poke through her pocketbook for what? Cigarettes? A tissue? Or both? She pulls out a book. "No, that's silly," her expression seems to say, "reading in a bar." The book's a paperback. She slips it back into her pocketbook. Not her pocketbook. Her handbag. And the book's a pocketbook. Not a paperback.

There's a difference. Or there once was. Or a least to me there once was and still is while to many people those two kinds of books might be and always have been the same. She looks at herself in the mirror facing the bar. The whole place is a bar but I'm speaking of the bar the people on the stools are sitting at. She has dark hair. Black. Dark eyes. Maybe black. Long body. Not long legs. Long body on top. Sort of short legs. Heavy legs. Big feet. Big for such short legs I mean. She looks at herself in the mirror again and sees me looking at her. She smiles. I smile. All in the mirror. She turns to me. "You caught me," she says. "And you caught me catching you," I say. "And you caught me catching you catching me," she says. "And you caught—" "No, where I said it is where it ends," she says. I think about that. "No need to think about it," she says. "Anyway, hey, how are you, what's doing?" I say. "Hi." "Hello. My name's Rip and this is my hand." We shake. "Is your name really Rip?" she says. "No, it's Kip." "With a K or a C?" "K as in Kip." "Kip's kind of a strange name for a man, though less strange than it would be with a C." "Actually my name's Tip." "Tip's an even stranger name than Kip with a K and much stranger than Rip, though Rip's the most potentially menacing name of the three." "My name's really Lip," I say. "Now Lip I like. A bit more sensual than Tip and much stranger and more sensual than Rip or Kip. But that the end of your names?" "No—Nip." "Nip's not as strange as Lip, though it is the most appropriate name of them all for this bar." "My name's really Zip." "Quickest of the ips, Zip, even if its number of letters is the same." "Whip's my name," I say. "Spelled with an H or without?" "With." "Then Whip's your most potentially menacing name so far and also the longest of them all ending with ip." "No, my name's Pip." "Pip of a name Pip, but what really is your name as long as we're speaking of it? Let's skip Skip and I don't flip over Flip and I doubt if it's Drip." "Sip." "As appropriate for this place as Nip or Clip, though I don't think it's your real name." "My real name is." "Yes?" "Is." "Yes, what is your name, sir, please tell me your name?" "What's yours?" "Darlene." "Hello, Darlene." "Hi, Name." We shake. "Can I buy you a drink, Darlene?" "No, but may I buy you a drink, Name?" "Yes." "Do you come in here often, Name?" "Yes. But more often most recently, as lately I don't have much to do late at night. Or rather, I'm a little too much by myself these days late at night. Or rather, something else." "Spill it, Name." "I'd like to and also to leave this place, Darlene. Would you?" "With you?" "Yes." "No need to think about it. Lead." "Where would you like to go?" "Let's decide outside."

We go outside. "It's raining," she says. It isn't. "Why'd you say it's raining when it isn't?" I say. "Because somewhere it's raining," she says. "How do you know?" "I don't." "Then why'd you say it?" "I didn't." "You're a liar, Darlene." "I am. And you're right. There is a possibility it isn't raining somewhere now, and wasn't raining when I said it was before. A very small possibility, but one nonetheless, which I guess makes me a liar. You want to stay here or walk?" "I've walked a lot tonight, Darlene. I'm tired." "What do you do?" "Did I do to get tired?" "Did and do?" "I thought up and think up names for myself." "What name did you start off with before you started thinking up names for yourself, Name?" "Is your name really Darlene, Darlene?" "My name is a mystery to me." "And that, Darlene, is a mystery to me." "I meant by that, Name, that it's a mystery to me why I keep telling people my name's a mystery to me while I'm still able to tell people my name's Darlene." "I like the name Darlene, though you ought to change it." "Since you're the name expert, Name, why don't you change it for me?" "Change it to Darlene." "You like Darlene?" "A little more than I like the name Darlene." "All right, I will. From now on you call me Darlene. Now where do you want to go, Name?" "You tell me first, Darlene." "You know, I'm beginning to like the name, Darlene. Yes. It fits." "We can always go back to the bar," I say. "Let's. And it's also a good idea because I didn't pay for my drink or the one I never ordered for you." "The one you were going to buy me and still plan to?" "No."

We go into the bar. The bartender comes over and says "You forgot to pay for your drink, Darlene." "He called you Darlene," I say. "Oh, it isn't?" he says. "What's your name then, because I always thought it was Darlene." "My name's Darlene," she says. "Oh, Darlene," he says. "And his name is Name," she says. "Oh, Name." "And her name was Darlene," I say. "Darlene. Was. Now I got it. Well, what will Darlene and Name have to drink?" "What's your name, Ted?" she says to him. "Bartender." "I thought your name was Ted." "No, Bartender. I've always answered to Bartender." "That's true. You know, it's raining out, Bartender," she says. "Raining? Odd, but it doesn't sound or smell like rain. Look like it either. No drops or rain sounds and smells and it also looks like it's not raining." "Somewhere it's raining," she says. "Somewhere it probably is." Why do you both think that?" I say. "I was just agreeing with Darlene." "Why do you automatically agree with me?" Darlene says to him. "That's what I usually do at the bar." "You ought to change that habit," she says. "I'll think about it." "No need to think about it. I was wrong about the rain, which makes you doubly wrong in automatically agreeing with me and two, saying it's probably raining somewhere." "Well somewhere it probably is," he says. "You're probably right," she says, "which makes you doubly right in not automatically agreeing with me." "No, I think you're wrong there," he says, "but what'll you two have?" "Same," she says. "Same as hers," I say. "Two sames," he says. "Makes mine a double," I say. "You want a double too?" he says to Darlene. "Single," she says. "One single and one double same coming up," he says. He goes. "I don't really want a double," I say to Darlene. "I only ordered one because I never ordered one before." "Cancel it then." "I will." "You have to do it quickly, as I might be paying for your drink." "Cancel my double same," I say to Bartender, "and make it a triple." "We don't have glasses large enough for triple sames," he says. "You want a double and single glass to make up a triple?" "No, I don't much like drinking the hard stuff," I say. "Cancel my triple same." "And cancel my single same." "One triple and one single same canceled. Want a wine or beer?" he says. "Let's go outside," Darlene says to me. "See you, Bartender," I say. "See you, Name. See you again, Darlene." "Hope so," she says.

We go outside. It's raining. "It's raining," I say. "Probably somewhere it is," she says. "No now. Right here. It just started. Why do you always assume it's probably always raining somewhere?" "I'll tell you why, Name. Sit down. I want to tell you the story of why I assume it's always probably raining somewhere or at least that during every moment of the day there's more of a possibility it's raining somewhere than it isn't. Go on, sit." "The ground's too wet from the rain," I say. "Then can I at least assume it was raining somewhere before?" "You can and also can assume more than just that it was raining somewhere before." "Then I needn't go on with my story," she says. "I don't see why not." "Then I wish you'd sit down so I can tell it." "Honestly, Darlene, I would sit down if the ground wasn't wet from this rain." "This rain?" "The rain now and all the rain from before on the ground where you want me to sit." "If it was wet from someone spilling pan after pan of water on the ground, would you sit down?" "No." "Then wet from some nice little kid watering the ground with a hose?" "On the same spot you're asking me to sit down?" "Yes." "No, I wouldn't sit down, Darlene." "You don't want to hear my story then?" "Not true. I do." "Then sit down." "I will. Though somewhere else where it isn't wet where I sit down, or here once the rain stops and the ground dries. What you can do, if you don't want to go someplace where it's dry or wait here till this ground dries, is tell me the story inside the bar." "Good idea. Because I still haven't paid for my first drink from two times ago in there and because I definitely want to tell the story more than I don't. Where I tell it makes no difference to me, though it does seem to make a big difference where you hear it." "Would you tell it sitting down on the wet ground while I stand out of the rain?" "No." "Then let's go inside." "Yes."

We go inside. "You know, there were two people in here a short while ago who looked just like you two," Bartender says. "Were their names Darlene and Name?" Darlene says. "That's right. In fact, they were in here twice before." "Why do you assume that?" she says. "Because I saw them and they looked exactly alike both times." "Those could have been their twins you saw the time before last," she says. "Or their triplets, if you're all triplets. Triplets having drinks with triplets and all three women triplets named Darlene and the men Name." "You'd think their parents not only had a problem in raising and recognizing them," I say, "but in naming them though not in remembering their names." "You'd think so," he says, "and I'd in fact think you'd know so."

"Bartender," someone else says, "a rum on the rocks please?" "That's Someone Else," I say. "Well I have to get him a drink," Bartender says. "What'll you two have?" "Same thing Someone Else is having," I say. "I'll have what the previous Darlene had," Darlene says. "The previous Darlene canceled her order," he says. "Then I'll cancel my order," she says. "Say, Bartender," Someone Else says, "my rum on the rocks?" "You still want the same?" Bartender says to me. "Same." "Same for me too," Darlene says, "as I never canceled a rum on the rocks before." "Three rum on the rocks coming up," he says. He starts making our drinks. "Do we really want rum on the rocks?" Darlene says to Bartender. "I don't," he says. "Neither do I," she says. "Cancel two of those rum on the rocks," I say. "Don't cancel mine," Someone Else says. "Only cancel one then," I say. "I'll have a white wine," Darlene says. "Just like the first Darlene ordered and had and never paid for," Bartender says. "What's all this about other Darlenes?" Someone Else says. "A name game they and now I have going," Bartender says. "That's Darlene." "And that's part of the name game?" Someone Else says. "You see, her name wasn't originally Darlene, but Darlene." "Now I don't get it." "Pay close attention. She's Darlene, but she hasn't always been. And he's just Name and for as long as I know him, always has been." "Then he's the game or Game's his last name. Though Game can't be his last name, as you said his name's just Name." "As far as I know, Just isn't his first name and Game isn't his last. His name's Name and he's only part of the game, just as you and I are. I'm Bartender." "You mean, you are a bartender." "I'm also a bartender." "What else you do?" "I do lots else, but the only thing I do professionally is tend bar." "I still don't see what your being a bartender has to do with their name game or Name Game here or Just Name or just Name and Darlene over there other than talking about it with them and in the process trying to explain it to me, maybe even making the game even more complex than it started out to be." "That's almost the truth." "Well when you get the truth altogether, could you let me have it?" "You hear that?" Bartender says. "Someone Else just extended the game in a way we haven't thought of." "Now I get it," Someone Else says. "I'm

Someone Else and what I asked from you before and still haven't got is the truth. And he's Name and she's Darlene, though her name was probably recently changed to Darlene from Darlene, and you're Bartender and a bartender and the guy next to me could be called Guy Next to Me." "The Guy Next to Me," The Guy Next to Me says, raising his glass to Someone Else and Bartender and Darlene and me. "I don't have any truth to raise," Darlene says. "Three truths still coming up," Bartender says. He gives Darlene her truth, gives Someone Else and me the truths he was making before, and pours some soda water for himself and raises his glass. "That's not truth," The Guy Next to Me says to Bartender. "They hold me to one truth an hour, since they don't think I can mix and serve them up straight if I have more." "Even when a customer's buying you one and for everybody else here?" "You saying you're paying for my next one?" a woman two stools away from him says. "You're Everybody Else Here?" The Guy Next to Me says. "I thought she was A Young Lady Further on Down the Bar," Someone Else says. "To me she was a Drinker with a Big Tab," Bartender says. "No, I'm Everybody Else Here," she says. "Then I'm buying yours and one for the rest of them here," The Guy Next to Me says. We look around. There's no one else left in the bar. "Okay," Bartender says, "one more than I'm allowed for the hour," and pours himself the same truth Darlene has and mixes another one for Everybody Else Here. We all raise our truths and Someone Else says "What should we drink to?" "To truth," The Guy Next to Me says. "We drink truth, not to it," Bartender says. "Then let's drink to it," Darlene says. "To it," we all say. We drink. I finish my truth, say goodnight and leave the bar. It's stopped raining. I head for home. "Name?" I hear behind me. I keep walking. "Name. Your name's Name, isn't it?" Darlene says, catching up. "We drink and drank to it," I say. "Yes?" "I'm saying—" "Yes?" "Yes," I say. "Good," she says.

On our way to my building she says "Incidentally, what is your name?" "Name." "That's your real name." "My real name is Name." "Then so is mine." "That's a coincidence," I say. "And I like your name," Name says. "I like your name too," I say. "I not only like your name but I like you, Name." "I like you too, Name." "This is really unusual. Because there probably aren't two people with the same name as us and feeling quite like us about our names and each other anywhere in the world right now." "I don't know why you assume that." "You don't think there's a reason?" "No." "I do."

STREETS

Two people stand on the street corner. Or rather she stands on the corner. He's gone into the corner store. She looks up. A jet plane passes. She waves at the plane and laughs. She looks at the cars passing on the avenue. A bus. She waves at the people in the bus. A young boy in the bus waves back. She sees me waiting at the bus stop. She smiles. I smile. The man comes out of the store. He holds out a package he didn't seem to have when he went into the store. She takes the package and puts it in her pocketbook and runs. He walks after her. She sees him walking after her and runs faster. He starts jogging after her. She sees him and begins to run as fast as she can. At least it seems like that. She's sprinting. He's now running after her. She turns around as she runs and sees him gaining on her. She seems to try to run faster than she was going, but she can't. She's in fact slowing down. She's getting tired. The pocketbook she's holding might be heavy. I'm running along the avenue behind both of them. People turn as we run past. They look at the couple and then me as if I know what's going on. I don't. As if I'm part of a threesome—this woman, man and I—but I'm really not. I was just watching them on the corner. Then just the woman on the corner. Then the man leaving the store and holding a package out to her and the woman taking the package and putting it in her pocketbook and running away with it and the man following her, and now he catches up. He tries to take her pocketbook. She pulls her pocketbook back. I stand and watch this from about fifteen feet away. Other people watch. He pulls the pocketbook from her. When she tries to get the pocketbook back, he pushes her. She falls. A man steps over to them and says something to the man who pushed her and holds out his hand to the woman and pulls her up. The man with the pocketbook tells him to mind his own business. The helping man steps back but continues to watch them while sitting against a parked car. The man he's watching pulls the package out of the pocketbook and puts it in his side jacket pocket. The woman reaches into the pocket. He slaps her hand. She slaps his face. He punches her in the face. She falls, this time on her back. Her head hits the ground hard, and she seems unconscious. The helping man rushes over and begins arguing with the man who hit the woman. The man swings the pocketbook at him and catches him in the face. The woman was only stunned or maybe unconscious for a few seconds. The helping man has a cut on his cheek from the bag. He pulls out a knife. The other man tries to knock the knife out of his hand with the pocketbook, but the strap breaks and the pocketbook drops to the ground. The woman takes a handkerchief out of the pocketbook, presses it against the back of her head and stands. The two men are facing one another and shouting, the helping man waving his knife in the air, the other man his fists. "Use it. You just try and use it," he says to the man with the knife. Several people come over, and others from across the avenue, and almost all of them crowd around the two men and the woman, though giving them plenty of room to move around. I still haven't moved. The crowd forms quickly and so densely around the trio that I can no longer see what's going on. I hear screams. From women and men. One woman turns around from the crowd with her wrist to her lips and looks at me and walks away. Her space is taken immediately, so I still can't see what's going on. I go over to the crowd, try to get a place in the circle by squeezing between two people, then look over a couple of shoulders to see what's going on inside. The man who tried to help the woman has his own knife in his chest and is lying on his back. The woman is lying on her front, her face on its side. Blood frames the back of her head, though it could be from the second fall that I saw. The man who hit her then is on his knees. Blood seems to be blotting his dark shirt around his stomach where he's holding himself.

"What happened?" I say to a man.

"Don't you see?"

"But how'd it happen?"

"What's the difference how? It's happened."

"Someone should go for the police."

"Good idea. You go."

"And the people there should be helped."

"That's what someone else said. You help them."

"How can I if I'm going for an ambulance and the police?"

"That's true. And an ambulance. You're right. They need one."

"Will someone please go for an ambulance and the police while I try and help these people?" I say.

"I'll go," a girl says. She doesn't look older than eight.

"Someone older?" I say.

There are about twenty people around the trio. Nobody responds to anything I say with even a head shake. I push through the crowd. The man's shirt is soaked now and he's groaning. The man with the knife in his chest looks dead. The woman is still bleeding from the head.

"Will someone please go for the police?" I say.

"Let the girl go," a woman says. "I know her. Know her mother, I mean. She's a smart girl. Rather, her mother says she's smart."

"She's smart," another woman says. "Go, girl. Call the police."

"I need the money," the girl says.

I put my hand in my pants pocket. Everyone watches me go through all my pockets for change. I look at the crowd nearest the girl. "I thought I had change," I say.

"Sure," a man says. He gives the girl a dime.

"Give her two," a woman says. "She might lose the first."

"I won't lose the first," the girl says. "I know who to call and how. I dial. I put the dime in."

"You put the dime in and then you dial," the woman says.

"I know, I know. I only need one dime." She goes.

I get down on one knee. I don't know whom to help first. Probably the woman. The knifed man looks dead. If the knifed man is dead, and he didn't by some accident fall on the knife himself, then the man who stabbed him would seem like the last person to help. I'm not sure about that. All I know is someone has to be helped first. So I pick the woman. Maybe because she is a woman. Though if she's the one who stabbed the man, then I probably should first help the man who I thought stabbed the man in the chest, though only if I'm sure the stabbed man is dead. If he isn't dead, then I wouldn't know which man to help first— that is, if the woman is definitely the one who stabbed the man, but not out of self-defense. If she stabbed him out of self-defense or to protect the man who chased and hit her before, then the last person to be helped would be the stabbed man, dead or not, and the first would be either the woman or the man holding his stomach.

"Who stabbed who?" I say.

"Who stabbed who?" a man says.

"Who's responsible for all this?"

"I didn't see it."

"I did," a woman says.

"Who stabbed who?" I say.

"Why you want to know? You a cop?"

"No. I just want to help these people."

"You a doctor?"

"I'm a passerby, just like you."

"No you're not. You were running after them before."

"I was running after them because I saw the man chasing the woman, and I thought something was wrong."

"Something was," a man says.

"What happened?" I say.

"You're the one running after them, and all of a sudden you didn't see?" a woman says.

"No."

"Like hell you didn't."

I decide to help the knifed man first. At least I can find out quick enough if he's dead or not. If he's alive then there can't be much I can do for him except put a support under his head, and then I can go right to the woman or other man.

"Will someone please do what they can to make the woman and that man comfortable while I see to this one?"

"Best medicine and treatment in these situations is to wait for professional help," a man says. "Real doctors or hospital aides, but someone ignorant of medicine can do more damage than someone not doing anything."

"He's right," several people say in different ways.

"But I know what I'm doing. I'm not in the field of medicine, but I know how to stop someone from bleeding to death."

"How?" a man says.

"Tourniquets, for one thing."

"That's for arms and legs, not the head."

"I said 'for one thing.' Another way is pressure points. The neck. There's one there. They're all over the body. Or you stick your finger on the wound or in the blood vessel that's cut if you can't find the right pressure point. At least let me try."

"Sure, we can let you try, and watch you finish off all three of them before our eyes. Just stay off them."

"I'm sorry, but I still think it's best I try." I feel the woman's forehead. Put my ear next to her mouth. "She's breathing."

"We said stay off her," the man says. "Wait for help."

"What I think is someone else ought to call the police for help. That girl might have met a friend or someone and just forgotten about it."

"She's a good trustful girl," the woman who said she knows the girl's mother says.

"I'm not saying she's bad or distrustful. But younger people— particularly around her age, eight or nine or so—do get distracted more than adults."

"She's ten," the woman says.

"Ten-year-olds probably get less distracted than eight- or nine-year-olds, but still get distracted a lot."

"So do adults," a woman says.

"I know. But children more so."

"Children more so. You're right. Maybe someone ought to go as he says. You go, why don't you?" she says to me. "You seem so interested and reliable."

"I want to stay here and help these people now."

"I think you'd best be giving help by phoning for it than touching them," a man says. "And out of all of us, you're the one who seems more liable to do the most trouble if you stay."

"I agree," a woman says.

"I don't." I feel the stabbed man's temple. "He's alive."

"Too bad," a man says.

"What are you saying?" someone else says.

"What I said. Too bad he's alive. He started it, didn't he?"

"No, the other man did."

"It was a woman," a woman says. "She stole something from the man with the knife in him. That's why he chased her. The other man just happened to step in. And she took the knife out of his hand, which he only pulled out to protect her, and put it in the stabbed man's chest."

"I think the woman and the man holding his stomach did know one another," I say.

"You know them?"

"I saw them together. They were standing on the corner of this same avenue three blocks away. The man went into a corner store, and the woman waited for him outside."

"What kind of store?"

"I forget. A jewelry store. I was waiting for my bus. Then the man came out and held the package out for her, or just held it out without any intention of giving it to her. Anyway, she took it and put it in her pocketbook and ran. The man walked after her. She ran faster. He started jogging and then ran after her. She at first ran faster than him when they were both running, and then, because she was tired or her pocketbook had become too cumbersome to run with or something, she slowed down and he caught up. Right here. I was standing over there. Next to the hydrant. The one where the two dogs are."

I'm still on one knee and now pointing through someone's legs. Almost all of them turn to look at the hydrant and dogs. "Then the man took the pocketbook from her, and she tried getting it back. He pushed her and she slapped him. Rather, he hit her hand and she slapped his face and he punched her and she went down. That's when the man who was knifed stepped in for the second time. Most of you must have seen that. The first time he stepped in he was told to mind his own business and he did. This time I don't remember him being told anything. They just argued. And he pulled out a knife—the knifed man did—after the other man hit him in the face with the pocketbook. Then the other man must have taken the knife away from him and stabbed him with it, though I'm only assuming now, since that's when you all suddenly encircled them and I couldn't see what happened."

"That's not at all what happened," someone says.

"Then what really happened?" someone says.

"You didn't see it?"

"I just got here."

"Remember that little girl who went to phone the police?"

"I told you, I just got here."

"Well, there was a little girl of about nine or ten or so who we sent to call for help."

"Ten," a woman says.

"Ten. Well, she knifed him."

"Don't be ridiculous," several people say in different ways.

"I thought we needed a bit of, I don't know, levity here, what with the grim sight of them lying there and waiting for help taking so long. But I guess it was in bad taste."

"Very."

While they were saying all this I took my jacket off, rolled it up and put it under the woman's head.

"Here it comes," a man says.

We hear an ambulance siren and look in the street. The ambulance and police escort preceding it pass.

"Must be for someone else."

"I really think one of us should try and get the police now," I say. "Just to remind them, if the girl called, or to let them know, if she didn't."

"Maybe he's got a point," the woman who said she trusts the girl says.

"I'll go," I say.

"You've already done enough damage," a man says.

"What do you mean? You wouldn't let me do anything, which is why I'm volunteering to go."

"You picked up that woman's head just before. Maybe they didn't see you, but I did. And in her condition you might have done just enough damage to kill her, when if you hadn't touched her she might have been saved."

"You don't know that."

"I say we make sure he stays here and we send someone else to call."

"Send anyone you want, but I'm also phoning for help." I push through the crowd. I look back. The circle's together again around the three injured people. I go into one of the stores nearest the crowd and ask the hardware-store man if I can use his phone.

"There's a public booth a block north of here," he says.

"I haven't a dime and this is an emergency."

"All I get every day are people with no dimes and life-and-death emergencies."

"Let him use the phone," a woman at the cash register says.

"I said no."

"But it's real important. Can't you look outside yourself and see?"

"Just keep looking for your register-tape error and don't butt in."

"Don't you talk to me like that."

"I said shut up," he says to her.

"And I'm telling you this is as much my store as yours and even more so, as it's in my name. And I want him to phone for the police for whatever it is that happened out there."

"I better go somewhere else," I say.

"You're damn right," he says.

"No. Go no other place. Use our phone. It's mine—in my name—and in the back there, right down that aisle."

"Use the phone and you're flattened," he says, his hand in a tray of wrenches on the counter.

I head for the door. The woman runs after me. "I said you can use the phone."

"But I don't want to cause any more trouble and also get killed for it."

"Trouble between him and me is nothing new. Besides, he's a blow-hard—all wind and words. So use the phone."

"No."

"He's smart," the man says. "Here's a dime, sonny. Now get the hell out of here." He throws me a dime and I catch it.

"Coward," she says to me. "Idiot," she yells at him.

He picks up a wrench and comes over to her. "Don't be calling me an idiot."

"All right. I apologize. You're not an idiot." He relaxes both arms to his sides and walks away. "You're a big moron and stupid son of a bitch."

He rushes at her to hit her with the wrench, or it at least looks like that. She runs. I freeze. But I just about froze before and watched and now three people are near dead out there. The man runs past me after the woman. I grab the hand that holds the wrench. "Get his other arm and we'll trip him," I yell at her. He hits me on the back with his other arm or hand. I fall. He lifts the wrench over my head and yells "Meddler, meddler," and comes down on my shoulder with it and then my neck. Both times it seemed he aimed for my head. Something in me broke both times. He lifts the wrench again.

"Don't," she yells.

He turns to her. I start to crawl to the door. He comes after me.

"Leave him," she yells.

He turns to her. I'm still crawling. He steps over to me with the wrench raised.

"Stop," she yells.

He rushes her and hits her across the face with the wrench at the same moment she sticks a chisel in him. I don't see where she got him. Somewhere high up. They both fall. They don't make sounds. I crawl out of the store to the crowd. The ambulance and police still haven't come. I grab a man's ankle and shake it. He turns. "Oh my gosh," he says. "What happened?"

"In there." I can't point. "The hardware. Two people are hurt. Maybe dead. The man hit me twice with a wrench and then the woman with a wrench, but she much worse than me. She stabbed him to protect me and herself. Take care of her. Then me. The man should come third. Or rather, call the police, for I never could. Help for all six of us. I'm sure that girl never called. They would have been here by now."

"He wants us to phone for help," he says to the crowd.

"You go," a woman says to him. "He told you."

"I haven't any change."

"Use the phone in the hardware store," I say. "In back. Straight down the middle aisle."

"You don't need a dime?"

"Maybe you do. I thought it wasn't a pay phone, but maybe it is. But they must also have a regular business phone that doesn't take dimes."

"I better take a dime just in case."

"Two," I say.

"Two dimes then."

"Two ambulances. For the trio in the street and the couple in the store and me."

"The stabbed man doesn't need help anymore."

"The one in the street?"

"Maybe the one in the store also," a woman says.

"That would mean only four people need help," the man says.

"We'll still need two ambulances if they're the triple kind," I say.

"The lady doesn't seem to need help either," a man says. "The one in the street, I mean. She doesn't seem to be breathing."

"Check," I say. "No, just go in the hardware store and call the police. Don't tell them how many ambulances we'll need. The ones

I'm thinking of they might be out of. Just say six people are seriously hurt. Also, if some of you would turn me over now and put something under my head. A jacket. But gently. Rolled up, and not the jacket that's under the head of the woman in the street."

"I wouldn't touch him," a man says. "You might do more damage than not."

"Don't worry," I say. "I'm uncomfortable, in pain, and know what I need. I give you permission."

"For his own good I wouldn't touch him. His shoulder seems broken. So does something with his neck the way he's keeping it."

"Wait for the ambulances," several people say in different ways.

"Phone," I say to the man.

"I don't want to go in the store. The man with the wrench might be up and ready to clip the first one to come in. For all we know, you could have been the one who provoked him into using the wrench, and he might think the next person to come in his store is the same."

"I didn't provoke him. I only went in to call."

"Maybe you're right. The courts will decide if it has to come to that. But I'm not going in there. Anyone know where the nearest phone booth is?"

"Three blocks south on this avenue," someone says.

"One block north," I say.

"The dime," he says. "I'm all out."

Several people search their pockets and handbags.

"In my shirt pocket," I say. He takes out of my pocket the dime I was going to call with before and goes. "I think someone else should go in the hardware store to also phone the police and see about the couple."

"You think he's going to get distracted like that ten-year-old girl?" a woman says. "He's a grown man."

"I know. But I'd like the double assurance that help will come."

"Look. I know him a long time, that fellow who went. When he says he'll do something, he does it."

"That's not the way I see him," a man says. "He's owed me ten dollars for two years now and always says he's paying up and never does. I've given up on him and don't even ask him anymore."

"Well, I know him as a very dependable honest man," she says. "Always pays his rent on time. Never a bill due on anything for more than a day or so."

"Not him. Two years he's owed me. For supplies."

"Then you better go in the hardware store and call the police," I say to this man.

"Right." He goes into the store.

"You know who you just sent to call the police?" a man says to me. Several people laugh. "The worst thief of them all. He's going to steal from that store everything that isn't held down."

We hear sirens. It seems the ambulance is going to pass. A man runs into the street and waves at the ambulance to stop. It's gone.

"Someone else again must be sick or in trouble," a woman says.

"Or that siren's on just so they can get through the traffic quicker," a man says. "They have that advantage over most of the other cars and use it."

I turn myself over on my back.

"You shouldn't do that," a man says. "You can hurt yourself worse."

I put my good arm under my head. Everything hurts. "You know, it's possible those people who went to phone could all be unreliable." I say. "I think someone else should call."

"How many do you want?" a woman says. "If they are reliable and too many people phone the police, they'll think we're cranks or crackpots and never send anyone to help. Three's enough."

"Three are plenty," a man says.

"Three for what?" someone new in the crowd says.

"Three people have gone to call the police for these four people in the street here and a couple who are seriously hurt in the store."

"Three calls are more than enough," the new person says.

I shut my eyes and wait.

About the Author

Stephen Dixon is the author of more than 125 published short stories. They have appeared in magazines as varied as *Harper's* and *Playboy, Paris Review* and *Fantasy and Science Fiction.* His previous books are *Quite Contrary* and *No Relief,* collections of stories, and *Too Late* and *Work,* both novels. Born and raised in New York City, Dixon graduated from City College of New York and has worked as a newsman, magazine editor, technical writer, and teacher.